DIFFERNT SIDES

PHANTOM SECURITY: BOOK ONE

MARISSA DOBSON

Published by Dobson Ink
Printed in the United States of America
ISBN-13: 978-1-946474-03-2

Acknowledgements

With every book there are a bunch of people behind the scenes to make it shine. My wonderful editors Molly Daniels and Natalie Owens. Codi Johnson for beta reading and for loving the characters as much as I do. My proofer, Brynna Curry, for your amazing support through everything.

My assistant, Teresa, who has nagged me for a year to write *Protecting Forever* (Forever Creek Shifters) but understood my muse wouldn't allow me to devote myself completely to anything else until *Different Sides* was finished. I hope you enjoy *Different Sides* until I can get *Protecting Forever* complete.

To my readers, you're the reason I can do what I love. No words can ever express how grateful I am to you. You allow me to bring my characters to life and tell their stories. Each and every one of you are amazing. Thank you for your support.

Last but not least, my wonderful husband. Thank you for all your support.

True love finds a way.

Chapter One

Law and order had been drilled into Elise Dalton's head since she was old enough to understand what it was. According to her father, being the daughter of the chief of police left her with a bigger responsibility. She was supposed to set an example. Live her life on the straight and narrow—and for the most part, she did. The only time she took the detour road was for the man she thought she'd spend her life with—Flash Arquette.

During the freshman year of high school, the Arquettes had moved down the block from her and shook up the once quiet, small town. Mr. Arquette was a drunk who thrived on trouble and violence. If he wasn't causing a disturbance at the town's only bar, he was at home beating his sons, Rocco and Flash. How many times had her father locked Mr. Arquette up? Each time, his sister, who lived a couple of towns over, would come and take care of the boys until he was released, only to have the cycle repeat itself within a few weeks.

Now, standing in the front yard of the house she grew up in, she glanced toward the old Arquette place. Twilight was quickly turning to dark, making it hard to see anything except the outline of the house. No one had lived there in years and in the day, the neglect was clear. Tall grass, weeds growing through the cement driveway and around the walkway, the broken window, and missing siding made it clear to anyone that it had been abandoned for years. Just glancing at it made her wonder why her father hadn't done something all those years ago. Maybe if he could have locked Mr. Arquette up for longer than a few days, the boys would have had a fighting chance. Maybe their aunt would have taken them in and raised them right. If only her father had acted more on the situation, maybe he'd still be alive.

Silent tears rolled down her cheeks while inside, her temper raged. She wanted revenge but she could almost hear her father's words in her ear. *Let the justice system do what it's intended to do. It takes time but it works.* Did it really? If so, it would have saved the Arquette boys. It would have given Mrs. Arquette justice. And Flash…

"Ms. Dalton?"

Hearing her name spoken brought her out of the past. She glanced in the direction of the sound. A sleek black town car was parked at the end of the driveway but it was the man getting out who caught her attention. His sun-kissed skin and black wavy hair reminded her of someone she couldn't place—though the perfectly tailored suit, and the fact he was being driven by a chauffeur, told her he didn't belong there.

"Ms. Elise Dalton?"

"It's a bad time. You'll need to come back…" She wanted to say 'never' but she doubted that was an option. Whatever this man wanted, she didn't have time for it. She had just come from the funeral home where she'd made plans for her father's funeral. Right now, all she wanted was to be alone, not to deal with people. She took a step back toward the house, quickly finding her key.

"I only need a moment of your time." His voice sounded closer, nearly right behind her, but she didn't turn back to look.

"I don't know who you are, but right now I don't care. I've asked you to leave once and if you're persistent I'll have to call my fa…" Tears sprang to her eyes as she slid the key into the lock. Silently, she fought back the tears, refusing to cry in front of him.

"Elise—"

"I told you, now's not a good time." The door opened and she stepped into the doorframe, forcing herself to look at him. His brown gaze caught her attention and for a moment she thought she was looking into someone else's eyes.

"Five minutes, that's all I need." Stepping closer, he placed his hand on the door, crowding her space.

"Fuck, man! Don't you get it? I can't do this now. I just…he's…"

"I get it, but I have a message that can't wait."

The anger over this man's persistence was quickly being replaced by fear. Something about a message made her want to reach into her bag for her gun. She wasn't on duty so she hadn't put her gun on her belt. Instead, she'd left it in her bag.

"Are you listening to me?"

She swallowed the lump in her throat. "I don't want any trouble." Her father was dead; why would anyone be after her? She had nothing to do with whatever he was investigating. They might have been in similar career fields but they didn't discuss their work. They were both committed to their jobs, often bringing their work home with them, but it didn't impact their time together. Hell, she hadn't even been in town in over a week. *I missed the last days of his life…*

She watched the man's lips move but her brain refused to focus until the last word. *El.* "What did you say? What did you call me?" Her knees went weak, forcing her to wobble and take a step back to regain her footing.

"You need to sit down. Let me help you inside." He grabbed hold of her arm and she went stiff under his touch. "You don't recognize me, do you? Shit, Elise, I thought you said you didn't want any problems because you knew who I am."

"Sir." A bulky man in a dark suit came up the sidewalk toward the porch.

"Everything's fine. Watch the house. I'm taking her inside." Before she could argue, he swooped her into his arms and strolled into her house. He kicked the door shut behind him as he carried her toward the living room.

"Put me down," she demanded, even though she wasn't sure if she could stand. Her body felt as if it was liquid—nothing felt right.

He sat her down on the sofa and grabbed the patchwork quilt off the back, draping it around her shoulders. "I'm not surprised you still have this, but I *am* surprised you have it out. It must have driven your old man insane."

"You know…" Her words faded as he leaned over and flicked the light on. For the first time, she was able to completely take in the man before her and her gaze fell on the jagged scar across his cheek. "No…it can't be. Rocco?" Terrible thoughts crossed her mind as she realized Flash's brother was in her house. She quickly wondered if he was there to kill her before she realized she hadn't done anything wrong. She hadn't been in town when her father was killed, so they couldn't be concerned she'd been a witness to any of it.

"The one and only." He squatted down in front of her. "Flash called me."

"Flash…" She wasn't sure if she wanted to cry or scream at the mention of him; either way she wanted to do it alone. "I think you should leave."

"*I'm innocent, El, I swear.* That's the message I came here to deliver. That's what I tried to tell you earlier but I don't think you were listening to me. You just stared past me." He placed his hand over hers. "Elise, I'm truly sorry. This is one of those situations that all the money in the world doesn't fix. You have to know, I would if I could."

"Really? Because if you're in town, I'm betting you've hired a lawyer for him. A high-powered lawyer…someone who could get him off or at least procure a lighter sentence. You don't care about me or my father. You're only here to lighten the load on your conscience." She pulled her hand out from under his.

"You're damn right; I hired him a lawyer because—"

"I don't need to hear your excuses. He murdered a police officer and could be looking at the death penalty." Her chest tightened at the very thought but she forced herself to continue. "He's your family. I understand you want to save

4

him, but I don't need to hear it."

He rose to his feet, grabbing hold of her wrist and pulling her up with him. "Didn't you hear me when I gave you his message? He didn't do it."

"Bullshit." She tried to pull her wrist from his grasp but he held tighter.

"When have you ever known Flash to fight against the charges? Even the computer fraud charges, when we both know he didn't do that. A newborn baby has more computer sense than my brother."

"The evidence—"

"Is manufactured," he supplied before she could finish. "Flash would give his life to protect you. He wouldn't want to see you like this. Your old man could be an asshole, but he was your family. Flash respected that. Your father would have never approved of him and for that reason he took himself out of the equation so you wouldn't be hurt."

He broke my heart. Yet, she refused to admit that aloud. "It doesn't change anything."

"It changes everything."

"The evidence they have could put him away for life, if not land him on death row." She didn't want to admit it but if Rocco was telling her the truth, then her father might never see justice for his murder. He believed in the system. Now, if she believed the man standing in front of her, the wrong person was going to get convicted and her father's real killer would go free. She didn't know what to think.

"Elise, I know you're upset right now but before you allow this to erase the good times you've shared with Flash, give us time to prove his innocence."

"That's not how this works." She dropped down onto the sofa, forcing him to let go of her wrist, because her energy was gone. "You're not supposed to have to prove you're innocent. They're supposed to prove you're guilty beyond a reasonable doubt."

"Your father stood for the law and he taught you to believe in the system.

Now that you're older, you've had to realize it doesn't always work that way. The police here have been gunning for Flash for years. They've picked him up for little things, never the bust they want. Flash is far from innocent in many things, but murdering your father...no." He stepped back from the sofa.

"How can you be so sure?"

"Can't you trust me on this for now? I'll get you the proof. I just need some time."

She sat there in silence for a moment debating what he said before finally shaking her head. "No, Rocco, I'm sorry. I can't. My father was murdered; if not by him, then by someone else. If it really was someone else, he could be getting farther away as we speak. If you want me to believe you, then give me something—anything."

With every word, she could feel the desperation getting heavier. She wanted to believe him, she wanted Flash to be innocent, but she couldn't believe any of this on Rocco's word. She didn't know him well enough to know if he was lying. If Flash had been standing before her, she might believe it, maybe because she wanted him to be innocent—but more than that she'd know if he was lying to her. Years earlier, she realized he had a tell, allowing her to know whenever he was lying.

"Twenty minutes before the..." He paused, as if he didn't know what he wanted to call the murder of her father. "He was with me. A confidential business meeting. Shit, Elise, that's all I can give you. I'm in violation of my contract by telling you that much. I need a few hours and I'll have the red tape cleared enough that he'll be alibied."

"Twenty minutes before? Are you serious? That's not a strong enough alibi."

"It is when the meeting happened in New York. There was no way Flash could have gotten back into town in twenty minutes." He dragged his hand through his hair. "I pulled Flash into this because I needed his skills. It's going to save his life; otherwise they'd send him up the river until they could shove a needle in his arm, ending his life. Trust me when I tell you he's not just in this mess because of the life he's chosen to live. I've made enemies in my business and they can't come after me personally—I'm too well protected—so they go after the only one left to them."

"What kind of meeting?" she pressed, needing more.

He slipped his hand into his jacket pocket and ignored her question. "I've got someone working on the traffic cameras. They'll find further proof he wasn't anywhere near Pinewood when this happened."

"Roc—"

"Twelve hours." From his pocket, he pulled out a business card. "I need you to trust me for twelve hours and I'll have Flash out of jail. Once that's taken care of, I'll help you find the person responsible. My cell number's on the back; call me if you need anything. I'm staying in town until this matter is resolved." He started to walk away from her.

"You never answered my question."

"I can't." He glanced back at her. "Elise, you mean a great deal to my brother, and if I could tell you I would, but I can't. The information I've already told you puts us both at risk. Anything further would be disastrous. I can tell you this: the same organization that signs your check also signs the ones for me and Flash."

Without another word, he was gone, leaving her more confused than she had been. Leaning back against the sofa, she let the first tears fall. Her gaze scanned the pictures displayed above the fireplace but her mind couldn't focus on what she was seeing. She was too full of grief and unanswered questions to appreciate the memories called by the images before her. What the hell did Rocco mean? The same organization? That wasn't possible. Was it?

More confused than before, she pulled the quilt into her lap and stared down at it. The worn quilt had been her favorite since that rainy afternoon she'd spent making it with her mother. Dad had always thought it was precious to her because of the time she'd spent with Mom. Little did he know it was because of the small cloth squares. Each one represented a memory she'd made with Flash. Their first date, first kiss…she even had pieces of the shirt she'd worn as they were moving in to the house down the street. It was so full of memories and on every visit home, she used it. She always figured she chose to leave it there because it was where she could use it the most. After all, she spent more time in Pinewood than at her own condo, but now, she realized, it was a small jab at her father. To have this as a centerpiece of the living room and their time together was a reminder she never stopped loving Flash. He had always been there with her, even once he took himself out of the picture. She ran her fingers over the soft material. *How did things get so fucked up?*

It wasn't the first time Flash Arquette had found himself behind bars. Still, he flinched as the bars slammed shut behind him. With the life he lived, he'd expected to be back after his last stint in prison, but he never would have dreamed it would happen with a murder charge hanging over his head.

Most people in Pinewood considered him a good for nothing criminal but they didn't know him. Every decision he made seemed to be the right one at the time. If a woman was getting the shit beat out of her by some asshole, he couldn't stand around and do nothing. He'd seen it too many times when he was a child—when his father had beat his mother and he'd been too young to stop it. Now, he wasn't. It had cost him a few years in prison for attempted murder, but those years proved worth it when he found out the woman had managed to get out of the situation and was now living her life in Florida. If only someone could have helped his mother like that, maybe she wouldn't be dead.

"This place is a second home to you, isn't it, Arquette?" The guard chuckled as he removed the cuffs. "Get used to it. You're not going to slither away this time."

Glaring at the guard, he refused to comment. Anything he could say would make the bastard think he was getting under his skin. Everyone at Pinewood Police Department was pretty happy with themselves for taking him down, but soon they'd be put in their place. He had to trust Rocco and his people to get this taken care of.

The guard retreated, leaving him alone in his cell to think on his sins. He rubbed the red marks from the handcuffs. The metal cuffs were tight enough to dig into his skin but he refused to give them the satisfaction. "Fucking bastards."

The police force had fixed eyes on him for more than a year now, determined to lock him up before his crew had a chance to do any further damage to their peaceful town. Even the town residents had decided he was guilty, no matter the charges. Now they'd want his head. It seemed they weren't satisfied with him behind bars; they wanted him dead.

Prison was no easy ride, but it was part of his life. Before this mess, he would do his time without a fight. Not this time. This time, he was innocent— and this wasn't the kind of fake, meaningless claim half the people in prison made. No, this time he hadn't even been in town when the crime happened.

This wasn't just a small crime that maybe he'd do a few months or even years for. This was murder and they were already talking about the death penalty. Chief Dalton had been murdered in cold blood and they were pinning it on him.

"Fuck!" Anger overwhelming him, he slammed his fist into the cement wall. "El…" He sank down onto the small metallic frame with a worn-out mattress on top and allowed his thoughts to turn to Elise Dalton. *His* El, the only woman he'd ever loved.

Did she believe he was capable of the pending charges? They both knew he was capable of murder but did she believe he'd kill her father? No matter the cost to himself, he would have never done that to her. El meant more to him than his own life.

He wasn't sure if he was angrier about the police department trying to pin the murder on him so they could get him out of the picture, or whether the system both her and her father stood for was failing her when she needed it the most. She believed in the system and fought for justice, but now it was robbing her by arresting the wrong person. With him in jail, they weren't out there searching for the actual murderer. "I'm sorry, El."

Her father had never liked him. Flash had never been good enough for his daughter. He knew he didn't deserve El, but he loved her, and even though Chief Dalton had been determined to keep them apart, he couldn't stop them. In the end, it was Flash's own actions that caused him to lose her. She was his everything. The one soft spot he had. To this day—if she called him, he'd be there.

She needed him now more than ever, but where was he? Behind bars accused of killing her father. *I'm coming, El. Don't give up on me, sweetie.*

Chapter Two

Twelve hours. Elise couldn't sit there and do nothing. She wasn't sure if she actually believed anything Rocco said or if she was just trying to prove to her heart that Flash wasn't the man she had fallen in love with so long ago. If there was even the slightest chance that her father's killer was still at large, she had to know. Doing nothing could allow his murderer to get away and they might never be able to catch him.

Forcing herself to get off the sofa, she went to her go-bag, which was still sitting next to the door. She had been in Florida working on a case and the team had just arrived back to the hotel when the call came in. She had expected a few hours' sleep before they had to be back at the station; instead, she'd had to rush to toss her things into her go-bag to make the next flight. Unable to think straight, she wasn't even sure she'd managed to gather everything from her hotel room. All she remembered was throwing things into the bag. The one thing she did remember was grabbing her laptop before she rushed out the door. Most of her work could be done remotely; if the team needed her she could still be there for them. It would give her flexibly while she was in town tending to things.

A quick word with her boss and she was off to the airport. The team didn't have anything they couldn't handle; they'd be in touch when they did. She hoped her boss wouldn't take her off the case because she needed something to keep herself from drowning in her grief. For her, that would be work. Her career was all she had now.

Pulling her laptop from the bag, she also grabbed a pair of black yoga pants and tank top. She'd change, get a pot of coffee, and get to work. A long night of digging into Rocco's story awaited her. Her clearance would give her access to things the general public wouldn't have and her hacking skills would allow her to get whatever else she needed. When it came to giving her father justice, she was willing to break whatever laws she needed to. They could throw her in jail if they wanted, but she wasn't going to let them convict the wrong man.

"I'm sorry, Dad." She set the laptop next to the sofa and continued through the house toward her old bedroom, all the while mumbling to herself. "I know you'd be livid if you were here, but I can't allow them to do this."

She stood in the doorway looking into her old room. It looked the same as it had since she was in high school, and even though she had stayed in that room at least once a month since she left home three years ago, she felt as if she was being transported back in time. Memories of the night Flash had snuck in her window washed over her. That magical night was one of two firsts for them. The first time they made love and the first time he told her that he loved her. That special night had been burned into her brain. No matter what happened between them, she couldn't forget the love they'd shared then.

Dropping the clothes on the edge of the bed, she pulled the nightstand drawer out. Rather than reach inside, she reached under it, retrieving a cloth bound journal from yesteryear. Removing the elastic closure, she flipped through to find the only memory of their relationship she'd allowed herself to keep there. Everything else she had moved to her apartment, where there'd been no chance her father could find them.

She stared down at the picture. The lighting was dim, but she remembered that moment as if it were the day before. They'd been down at the railroad tracks with Craig Freeman and the girl he was seeing at the time. She couldn't remember the girl's name but it didn't matter; they didn't make it until the following weekend. What had led them to the tracks was something else she couldn't remember, but the memories of that day would stay with her until she took her last breath.

Now that she looked at the picture, she could see this had been the beginning of Flash's decent. In those days, he was going down the road that would separate them—nothing she could have done to stop him. He worked out and it showed; he was bulking up. That wasn't the only change within him; his attitude was growing darker. To her, he'd remained the same sweet guy, but when it came to others, she could see the change. *I was losing you then. I just didn't know it yet.*

Unlike the elastic band keeping the book closed, there was no closure when it came to Flash. He still owned her heart; only now she wasn't a teenager any longer and no matter how much she wanted to, they couldn't go back. He was a criminal, possibly a murderer, and she stood on the other side of the law. Their time had passed.

The same organization signs our paycheck. Placing the picture back in the journal, she sat it on the bed and stripped out of her dress to change. It was time for her to put her skills to use and to do some investigating. She'd find out what Rocco had hinted at.

A few minutes later, she sat curled up on the sofa with a steaming mug of coffee and her laptop. The journal and Flash's picture on the cushion next to her made her wonder about her motives. Was she doing this to give Dad justice or to prove Flash didn't do it? Could she handle it if what she found proved Flash had murdered her father?

The laptop barely came to life when the doorbell rang, forcing her to set it aside and answer the door. Before she did, she grabbed the journal and dropped it into her purse, which was now sitting on the floor by the sofa. As she neared the door, Rocco's words echoed through her thoughts. *The information I've already told you puts us both at risk…* Maybe she was overreacting, but that was better than being dead. Retracing her steps, she grabbed her gun which she had holstered and in her purse.

Whoever was there pressed the doorbell again. "I'm coming." Her heartbeat echoed in her ears and she forced herself to take a calming breath. If she was in danger, she wouldn't go down without a fight. She wasn't an easy target. She might work behind the computer more than some agents, but she still had to complete the same training. She could handle herself. *So could Dad though and look at him.*

Next to the door stood a small window that allowed her to look out without the person seeing her because the hall light wasn't on. Without the porch light on, she couldn't make out much more than a tall, male figure. She hadn't wanted company so she'd shut off the light, hoping anyone who stopped by would think she wasn't home. No such luck this time.

Keeping the chain on the door, she opened it. "Hello."

"Shit, I thought you weren't going to answer." Craig leaned forward, pressing his hand on the door. "We need to talk."

The stench of liquor drifted toward her. "Now's not a good time."

"Fuck, Elise." He stepped forward. "Don't do this. I…shit, I don't know who else to turn to. I need your help. Please." He glanced back toward the road and when he turned back to her, fear flashed in his eyes.

Maybe it wasn't the best move but she closed the door enough to pull the chain off before opening it again to allow him in. "What's going on?"

"Do you have a drink? I need…" He moved past her, farther into the house.

"Damn it, Craig, you don't get to stroll into my hom…" *This isn't home anymore.* Her chest tightened as she realized she'd have to sell the house. Without Dad, there was nothing left for her in Pinewood—nothing to bring her back once a month.

"I need a fucking drink!" He strolled into the kitchen as if he owned the place, opening cabinets, looking for liquor.

"Fine, one drink and then you're going to tell me what the hell you're doing here or you're going to leave." Slipping her holstered gun into the waistband of her yoga pants wasn't ideal, but it would have to work; she wasn't about to set it down. She went to her father's make shift bar on an old wooden cart along the far wall in the living room. "Whiskey, rum, or vodka?"

"Whiskey. A double." Craig dropped down onto the chair and shook his head. "He didn't do it. You have to know that."

"Funny, you're the second person to tell me that." Keeping an eye on him, she poured the whiskey. "Is that why you're here?" She went to him and held out the beverage to him.

"I'm here because…" He took the glass from her and took a deep drink. "Holy fuck, Elise, I was with him. They know…I know…it's a setup. Fuck, they threatened to take me down with him if I so much as opened my mouth. They pointed a gun to my head…I thought I was going to die."

"What are you talking about? You were with him when? Who had the gun?" She sat down on the sofa, grateful she'd had enough foresight to bring the whiskey with her. She wasn't a drinker but she needed it now. Without bothering with a glass, she brought the bottle to her lips and took a long drink, allowing the liquid to burn her throat.

Two people had now come to her, trying to get her to believe Flash was innocent. This set off alarm bells in her thoughts. The stories didn't seem to line up and if they were lying to protect Flash, they'd need to get their stories straight before they went to the police with them because so far, she wasn't convinced. They each seemed to give him an alibi but there was no way he could have been in New York and with Craig at the same time. So, what was the truth?

"Flash and I met up outside of Pinewood. We rode back to town together, intending to stop by his place and then hit the bar for a drink. We'd just turned into his drive when Lewis and Chang pulled their guns on us, demanding we dismount and get on the ground. Flash bitched they were just there to cause him more problems but I was in the dark. I'd seen Lewis a few hours earlier and things were fine but in that moment, he looked at me with such hatred." In one deep swallow, he finished his drink and reached for the bottle to fill his glass again.

"In a minute." She moved the bottle out of his reach. "I need the rest of the story, and then if you want to polish off all of the liquor in the house, be my guest.

"You believe me? You believe Flash is innocent? What am I saying—you have to believe me. You know he would never do that to you."

Hadn't Rocco said almost the same thing? Why was everyone else convinced and why was she so uncertain?

"They have to have evidence or they wouldn't have arrested him," she tried to reason but even to her own ears, it didn't sound convincing.

"He wasn't in town. Want proof?" He reached into his pocket and pulled out a black leather wallet.

The thing was worn around the edges but she recognized it immediately. If she opened it, the corner would have FA & ED etched into it. It had been her present to him for Christmas her senior year. Unable to stop herself, she reached for it and slid her fingers across the smooth leather. Her heart pounded double time in her chest. *He still carries it all these years later.*

"In the struggle, they dropped it. I don't think anyone realized it." He nodded to the wallet. "Open it. There's a receipt for the toll. He was in New York. Shit, Elise, I watched him come across the bridge; that's where we'd planned to meet up. Whatever he was there doing, he had to do it alone, but we had planned to go for a ride today, so I tagged along. I drove around some back roads while he was doing his business in the city. He texted me when he was heading back and we linked up again."

"Did you explain that to Lewis?" Lewis was ambitious and he would take over for her father, but she didn't want to believe he could have been

16

responsible for her father's murder. Or that he'd arrest someone to cover whatever happened.

"You're damn right I did, and he threatened to shoot me if I didn't keep my mouth shut." Leaning forward, he snatched the bottle out of her hands. "Our paths separated somewhat. We still catch up for drinks or to ride, but I don't know what Flash is into now. What I do know is he didn't do this."

She opened the wallet and there, staring up at her, was a picture of them. Not the picture she'd added to the wallet before she gave it to him, but one of them weeks before everything had gone to hell. The last picture they'd taken together. He was leaning against the short stone wall that lined the creek with her in front of him, his arms wrapped around her, holding her against his chest, his body arched forward, his head near the crook of her neck. Moments before, he had been kissing along her neck, whispering naughty things in her ear.

"It's next to the money." He nodded to the wallet. "What are we going to do?"

"I'm going to get to the bottom of this."

"You can't, Elise. Lewis is dangerous." Sitting the glass on the side table, he rose from the chair with the bottle still in hand. "I don't know what Flash did to him, but Lewis wants him. Your dad kept him in check. Now…"

She checked the receipt, noting the time, before closing the wallet and setting it aside. "That's all the more reason. Dad drilled his values into me all my life. I can't turn my back on this. I have to see it through to the end, no matter the cost. No matter what I find."

"Alvin wouldn't want you to do this if the cost was your life." He paced next to the coffee table, avoiding her gaze. "After today, I wouldn't put it past Lewis that he's done it. What if you digging into this costs you your life? Flash's life? Someone else's? Are you willing to live with the consequences?"

"And if I do nothing Flash will go to prison for a murder he didn't commit." She took the gun out of her waistband and sat it next to her before pulling her legs up onto the sofa and leaning back. "Craig, they want to go for the death penalty."

"Fuck!" He brought the bottle to his lips and took a long drink.

She didn't think she could say it better so she stayed quiet and allowed him to drown his pain in the bottle. If she could have done it, she would have, but the more evidence that dropped into her lap, the more she was willing to believe that Flash was innocent. She just needed to prove it. She needed evidence and then she could do something with it.

"Well, I'm not letting you do this alone. Whatever you need, you can count on me." He sat the bottle down on the coffee table and looked at her. "So, where do we start?"

"I'm going to do what I do best. I'm going to gather the evidence we need. In the meantime, maybe you should stay here. I mean…is there someone at your place waiting for you?"

He let out a light chuckle and shook his head. "Under normal circumstances, I'd think you were coming on to me and, Elise, trust me, that's truly an honor. You're a beautiful woman but I also know your heart belongs to Flash. We both might disagree with the choices he's made in his life, but we still love him. Just in different ways. He's like a brother to me." He sat back down and closed his eyes. "To see Lewis attack him while he was handcuffed brought something alive within me that I didn't know I had. Rage burned inside me. But Chang had me at gunpoint. What was I supposed to do?"

"You're doing it now." She went to crouch by his chair and laid her hand over his. "We're going to fix this."

"They bloodied him and then hauled him off. Who knows what else is happening to him now."

"Nothing," she reassured him. "Rocco was here earlier. Flash has a team of lawyers; they're working on getting him out. Now I need to do my part. I'm serious—you should stay here tonight. If Lewis finds out you've come here, it could mean trouble. Either way, it won't be long before he finds out and he's going to come for us."

"Oh, that's reassuring." He looked at her and shook his head. "I hope they don't let you comfort witnesses in the field 'cause, Elise, I hate to tell you but you suck."

"Thanks, asshole." She slapped his hand. "Thankfully I deal very little with witnesses. My skills are in a very different area and fortunately for us, it's the one we need. Now, if we're going to get him out, I need to start digging. Make yourself at home and you know where the guest bedroom is. Make sure you tell me if you need anything or if you think of anything else that might be helpful."

He waited until she was settled back on the sofa with her laptop before he said anything else. "You still love him, don't you?"

"I…" She stared down at the keyboard as if she had to think about it. In her heart, she knew the answer but she wasn't sure if she wanted to admit it aloud. Her chest constricted with the horrible accusation that he might be responsible for her father's murder. Maybe he wasn't but until she knew for certain, she couldn't allow herself to go down that road. She needed to keep her feelings for him to herself; otherwise, she'd end up hurt again. *What am I thinking? I'm already hurt.*

"That's answer enough." Craig glanced down at the bottle of whiskey on the coffee table. "What can I do to help?"

"Nothing."

"Mind if I finish this?" He reached for the bottle but didn't bring it to his lips as he waited for her to answer.

"Be my guest. There's another bottle in Dad's office." Hard alcohol always left her with a nasty headache the next morning, but looking at the dark brown liquid she was tempted to give in to it and allow it to carry her away for a few hours. Temptation called to her, teasing her with the idea of forgetting everything for a few hours, but the risk was too great. Instead, she pulled up the internet and took a deep breath. In the next few hours, she would learn the truth and no matter what she found, she knew it was going to kill a piece of herself. *Please, let me find what I need.*

Chapter Three

Hours passed and night turned into day before Elise was certain she'd found enough evidence to prove reasonable doubt. Reasonable doubt wasn't good enough for her. She needed more answers. She needed to know who killed her father. If she were honest with herself, she wanted a confession or at the very least, undeniable truth. This wasn't a case where the victim was a stranger; this was her father. She thought she'd understood what the victims' families went through before but now, she had a whole new understanding. Who knew what Rocco might have accomplished overnight—but either way it was time to pay a visit to the police station. She wasn't going there to see Flash. No, she needed to see Deputy Chief Lewis.

She slipped her laptop into her shoulder bag along with the printout of Flash at the tollbooth, five minutes before her father was murdered. She wasn't sure if she was going to confront him with it yet, but she wanted to make sure she had it. First, she needed to hear what he had to say. When they spoke the day before, her grief had her emotional and she didn't comprehend everything he said. Today, she was ready.

Before she left, she grabbed a piece of paper and wrote Craig a quick note. There was no doubt in her mind that he needed to sleep off the bottle of whiskey he'd drunk and there was nothing he could do to help. If he went with her, Lewis would clam up. She needed to do this alone—not in her official capacity, but as Chief Dalton's grieving daughter.

'Running to the station. Stay, we need to talk. I'll be back soon. Elise.'

Grabbing her things, she headed out to the garage before her courage could slip away from her. She stepped inside and her gaze slid over to her father's pickup truck. It was an older model but there it sat, looking as if he had just washed and waxed it, the sparkling blue shining like diamonds. He'd loved that old truck almost as much as he'd loved her. It was the same truck he'd courted her mother in when they were teenagers. No matter the fact that he could have afforded any new one he wanted with all the bells and whistles, he'd refused to give up that old truck. She touched the shiny chrome handle and knew if she opened it there would be a picture on the visor of her mom, dad, and her, a few months before Mom passed away. She also knew that if she started it, the engine would purr to life without a moment of hesitation and the old beast would run better than her rental car.

Temptation to hop in and take it for a spin formed in her gut, but it would only make her sentimental. The last thing she needed when she went in to face Lewis and the rest of the department was to be emotional. Emotions were already running high enough. Her hand dropped away from the door handle and she promised herself she'd drive it soon. The truck would allow her to feel closer to her father and she could find comfort in that.

Moments later, she was behind the wheel of her rental car, heading out of the little subdivision and into town. Her mind played over the conversation she'd have with Lewis. She hoped all the years they'd known each other would count for something and maybe she could get more information out of him. She needed to trip him up so she didn't have to reveal what she'd done to access the data she had. Hacking into the police department's files would land her in hot water if her bosses found out, but she did what she had to do to get her father justice.

She pulled out of the housing development and onto Pinewood Pike. Her shoulder ached, warning her something was off. Those who worked with her often enough teased her about her shoulder being her sixth sense but she knew enough to trust it. Glancing in the rearview mirror, she noticed the work van that was right on her bumper—the same one she'd picked up moments after she'd pulled out of the driveway. She was being followed. Lewis? A lump rose in her throat. If he suspected she was digging into her father's death, she wasn't sure what he'd do. Before her mind could come up with ideas, her cell phone rang.

She grabbed it from the pocket of her bag and glanced at the screen. *Williams.* A call from her boss wasn't something she could ignore, so she slipped the earpiece in her ear and accepted the call. She hated the earpiece but since she was in a rental car, her cell phone wasn't connected to the car's hands free calling. "Hello, sir. I was going to call you in a bit to let you know when I'd return. The funeral—"

"Pull over."

"Sir?" Her eyebrows knitted in confusion and she glanced back at the van again.

"You heard me, Dalton. Pull over." The van behind her flashed its lights. "I'm behind you and we need to talk. Privately."

"Yes, sir." Seeing a pull off area that hunters used during hunting season, she did as instructed. Her heart raced as she parked and climbed out of the car. Why was her boss here? And why were they meeting on the side of the road to talk privately? Nothing was adding up.

The van came to a stop next to her car, blocking it from view in case anyone drove past, and the vehicle's door slid open, revealing Supervisory Special Agent Williams. "Get in."

She did as he asked, catching sight of Mick Lee behind the wheel and Jac Armiger in the passenger seat. Two team members and her boss in Pinewood when she'd left them less than twenty-four hours earlier, in Florida, in the midst of an active case. "Sir, I don't understand. What's going on? Why are you here?

What happened to the case in Florida?"

"This took priority. I'm sorry to hear about your father. He was a good man." He slid the door shut and tipped his head toward a makeshift work station. "Sit, there's something you need to see."

"Thank you." She took a seat and waited. Her mind ran with fears of what this meant. Priority. Had they been investigating something her father was working on? Had her father been under investigation? This was the team she worked with. She thought she could trust these guys; shouldn't she have known?

"Chief Dalton was working with us." Williams pressed a couple of buttons on the computer and an image of her father and Lewis came up on the screen. "Not our team, but the FBI."

"What? Who? He never said anything."

"I can't answer your questions." Williams dropped into the metal chair next to her. "Not because I don't want to, but because I don't know. We didn't know anything about it until after you'd boarded the flight last night. We caught the next one and have been working around the clock, trying to get caught up. I'm going to have the information today if I have to go to D.C. and meet with Director MacArther myself."

"We'll get the information, Elise." Jac came from the passenger seat to crouch near the table. "We also know you've dug into it yourself. That's where you're going now, isn't it? To confront Deputy Chief Lewis?"

"I have to know."

"And you will." Williams clicked the next button, bringing up another picture. The image was grainy but she could clearly make out Lewis standing over a woman's body. There was too much blood for her to be alive, and Lewis held a bloody knife. "He's dangerous. This was one of the images received yesterday from Chief Dalton. Two hours before he was killed."

"Is this why my father's dead?" She stared at the photo. "Did...Lewis..."

"You've already gathered evidence Arquette didn't." Williams brought up a third image—the same one she had in her bag. Flash at the tollbooth.

"Then why is he still sitting in a jail cell? Why was he even arrested in the first place?" She glanced at her boss and, in a split second, decided she needed to be upfront with him. If they were here because of all this, then she needed their help. "I have a witness. He can alibi Arquette and they weren't even in town when the murder happened. Lewis threatened him, told him not to tell anyone, but he came to me."

"Craig Freeman?" Jac asked.

"How did you know?"

"We spotted them on traffic and surveillance cameras. We can trace their route until they arrived at Arquette's place where Lewis was waiting." Jac placed a hand on her shoulder. "We've been at it all night. If this actually happened, we're going to make sure the right man goes to prison for Chief Dalton's murder. You can count on us."

"If?" She glanced from Jac to Walliams. "What's that supposed to mean?"

"Nothing's for certain yet. Give us a little more time. Right now, I need you to hold off confronting Lewis. We need him to believe he's getting away with this. Otherwise, we'll ruin the case your father was building." Williams let out a deep sigh and shook his head. "Elise, I know this is hard but the whole mess is bigger than his murder. We need to wrap this up tight and take Lewis down for everything. Otherwise, people like Chang are going to walk free and pick up where Lewis left off. There are at least ten other lives that hang in the balance."

"Lewis is involved in a sex trafficking ring and prostitution. They're getting the girls hooked on drugs and then forcing them to work the streets in the city for more drugs. There's a monthly auction where they're selling these women to the highest bidder. They've been watching Lewis for months and they're getting close."

"What Jac is saying is, we need to you to hold off a little longer." Williams shut the laptop and looked at her. "They didn't want to bring you in on this because you're too close to the case but Jac convinced them otherwise. I knew you'd see the errors in the story and once Rocco Arquette came to you, he'd have given you enough information to spark your interest."

"How did you know Rocco came to see me? Have you been watching me?" Her emotions were off the chart but she grabbed on to anger and focused on that. "That's why you were there when I pulled out. That's why we're here now. How dare you!"

"Listen here, Elise, we were there for your protection. If Lewis suspects you know too much, he'll kill you. We weren't present when Rocco was there. We've only been surveilling a few hours, but long enough to know that Lewis has a man across the street watching you. The house is empty, it's about to go up for sale, and he's got one of his men in there. So, don't doubt that he knows Rocco has visited you and that Craig Freeman is still in your house."

"Then how do you know Rocco came over?" At the moment, she couldn't even focus on the fact Lewis had someone spying on her; she needed to know more from Williams. Then, she'd handle the other issue.

"You ran his name last night. Which leads me to believe he told you he works for us." He held up his hand before she could question that. "I can't confirm or deny that. I can say he isn't officially on the books and that he has some high connections within the department. Even with his connections, it's not going to be as easy as he wants to get his brother out of jail."

"So, they're just going to leave him there, even though you know he didn't do it?" She thought that everything she'd learned meant she'd be able to rescue Flash. Now she was starting to believe they were just going to leave him to rot in jail so their case wouldn't blow up on them. What was she going to do?

"They need more time to be sure Dalton is even dead." Jac squeezed her shoulder. "You know the system isn't quick. You've got to give it time to work. We're here and we're going to do what we can to speed up the process."

"Not dead? What the hell does that mean?" Her eyes grew wide and her mouth went dry. She wasn't sure her mind could even wrap around what they were saying. "No, this isn't possible. He was too badly burned to do a visual identification, but they matched dental records. Lewis had the report…"

"There are things that don't line up."

"What does that mean? If he's not dead, where is he? My father wouldn't just leave me to think he was dead. Damn it, I'm here grieving and planning a funeral. I deserve to know the truth," she ranted, her voice growing louder with each word. "How can Flash be in jail on murder charges if there's no murder? What the hell is going on?"

"There was a murder. I just don't know if it was Dalton." Williams slipped a flash drive into her hand. "This is everything we've found. The police reports are there. The body's descriptions don't match Dalton's. Little things, like his height, make me question it. We're going to find out the truth but until we do, you've got to go along with everything as you already are. If he's alive, I promise you we'll find him. Now we don't have a lot of time. Lewis no doubt knows you've left the house and it doesn't take much to figure out you'd go to the station. Lee and I will be watching. Mel's here, too; she's with the other team, catching up on the information they have. We'll be in touch soon."

"What about Jac?"

"I'm going with you." He slid a box out of his pocket and opened it. "You're going to need to wear this."

A diamond ring caught her attention and she was once again confused. "What?"

"With the situation, we've decided you need further protection. Jac's going to pretend to be your fiancé. Mel lent you her ring, so take care of it," Williams explained.

"Protection or a babysitter? If you don't trust me, then just say it."

"Did you know that I chose you?" When she shook her head, Williams continued, "I was at the academy when you were going through your training. When I saw what you were able to do, I pulled some strings to get you assigned to the team. I know you had hoped to stay out of the field, to let your computer skills keep you in the office, but you have more qualities than that. When you joined us you were nervous, but in the time you've been with us you've proven repeatedly what I'd seen in you that day. What I'm saying is I know you're a good agent. You wouldn't risk this case. So no, I'm not sending Jac in as a babysitter, but as protection for you. We can't afford to lose you."

"Lewis will come after you if he thinks you know anything and, Elise, he's not going to come alone." Jac took the ring from the box and held it out to her. "While the others will be nearby, they might not get to you in time to help. So, what do you say? Will you be my fiancée?"

She held out her hand. What choice did she have? If she didn't agree to it, Williams would make it a direct order. At least it was Jac and not Mick. Not that she and Mick had a bad relationship; it just wouldn't be as easy to fake an engagement with him as it would be with Jac. *Here goes nothing…*

Flash sat silently in the interrogation room, letting them question him again, but still not saying a thing. He hadn't even bothered to mention the fact that his lawyers weren't present for this interview, because he wasn't going to answer any of their questions. In the last twenty-four hours, he hadn't answered a single one they flung at him and he wasn't about to start now. Just a little longer and Rocco would get him the clearance he needed to give them his alibi and he could put this whole thing behind him.

"A confession would make this easier on you." Deputy Chief Lewis leaned in close. "You murdering son of a bitch, you took Elise's father from her."

He did his best to block out Lewis' comments but in his mind, he could picture El heartbroken as she grieved for her father. A fist slammed into the side of his head and black spots danced across his vision but he didn't budge. His hands were cuffed to the table, keeping him in place, but even if they weren't, going after Lewis wouldn't help get him out of jail; it would only add extra charges.

"If you still cared for Elise, you'd give her the closure she deserves and confess. Fucking worthless bastard. She deserved better than you, and with you in prison, it will slam that door shut permanently, just like Dalton always wanted."

The door opened behind them and Officer Chang stood in the doorway. "Sir, she's here, in the Chief's office."

She's here. My El is here. She wasn't there to see him, but knowing she was close made him want to get to her. With Lewis watching him, he kept his features stone cold as if he didn't care. If they'd take him back to his cell, he might be able to see her.

Knowing she was in the building, he wanted to pummel the shit out of everyone that stood in his way and go to her. Multiple charges of assault on an officer would be added but to see her for a moment would almost make that mad stunt worth it. He couldn't tell her everything he wanted to, especially not that he still loved her, but she had to know he didn't do it. She could hate him for breaking her heart because he was guilty there, but not for this. He couldn't stand the thought of her thinking he had murdered her father.

"We're not done here." Lewis stalked toward the door. "I'm going to get a confession out of that asshole."

Being handcuffed to the table left no alternative except for him to sit there waiting until Lewis or someone else returned, but it didn't mean his mind had to stay locked in that room. Licking his lips, he tasted blood, no doubt from his split lip, just one of his many injuries. Rather than let his anger continue to boil, he let himself think about happier times. A time before his rap sheet started. A time when his life had been his own, and El had been his. Before he'd fucked

29

everything up, their love had grown strong and not even her father could crush it. *No matter what you think of me right now, I still fucking love you, Elise Dalton.*

Chapter Four

Standing in her father's office was all it took for Elise to lose the hold on her emotions. Tears rolled down her cheeks before she could stop them. She had so many memories of being in the office, watching Dad do what he loved, and it seemed as if every one of them sucker punched her in the stomach. The pictures decorating the desk and the bookcase on either side of the window behind the desk were mostly of her, alone. The only one taken with both her parents sat next to the computer, so he could see it no matter what he was doing at his desk. As if to remind him why he continued to do what he did. His words echoed through her pain. *Ellie, if I can save one person from suffering the loss we did, then it was worth it.*

"Elise?" Jac's hand touched her shoulder. "We're going to figure out what happened."

She turned to him partially so she didn't have to look at the chair her father had sat on day after day and so she could look out the window toward the other officers. How many were teamed with Lewis? "If he's alive, he'd have called." She kept her voice low so no one could overhear them.

"Not here." Pulling her against him, he lowered his head to her ear. "Lewis is heading this way. Are you okay, to do this?"

She was as ready as she was going to be so she nodded but stayed in his embrace. The office door opened, but she couldn't bring herself to look up at the man she knew would be standing there.

"Elise, what are you doing in here?" he asked as he moved farther into the office, his voice hard. "Who's this?"

"I…" She took a deep breath, pulled herself away from Jac, and tipped her head toward the empty box she'd brought with her. "I came to clean out his office."

"I can have someone do that for you. You don't need to worry about that." He crossed his arms over his chest and watched her. "Now who'd you bring with you?"

"I'm Jac Armiger, Elise's fiancé." Jac took his hand that was resting lightly on her back and extended it to Lewis. "It's a pleasure to finally meet you, Officer Lewis. Elise has spoken of you often."

"Deputy Chief Lewis," he corrected sharply. "Obviously Elise left out a few things. Not surprising since she never mentioned a fiancé. Neither did her father." He eyed Jac, taking him in, and Elise knew he wasn't convinced.

"You know my dad." She gave Lewis a smile. "We were close and we couldn't break the news over the phone. He met Jac on a number of occasions. This was something that we wanted to tell him in person. This weekend…" She couldn't stop the tears from returning but it only helped to make her story more believable.

"We were planning a surprise trip down here on Friday, so Elise could tell him. Then this happened," Jac explained as he wrapped his arm around her shoulders.

"Where were you yesterday?"

"Lewis, you know I was out of state for work and I flew out immediately. Jac came as soon as he could." Lewis's questions were making her uneasy, but she needed to stick with it.

"I'd have been here sooner if I could." Jac slid his fingers over the curve of her shoulder, keeping in his role. "What matters is that I'm here and she doesn't have to go through this alone. You don't have to worry about her and can focus on finding the person responsible for this tragedy."

"I have the bastard and I'm going to see that he fries for what he did. If I could, I'd burn that bastard alive like he…" Lewis shook his head and glanced back at her. "You know I'm not going to let that asshole get away with his murder. Your dad was a good man. This department is what it is because of him. I owe him for so much and now this is my only way of repaying him. That and making sure you're okay."

"Just make sure he gets justice." She stepped over to her father's desk and picked up a picture of them that past summer. "You're sure Flash is responsible for this?"

"You're damn right I'm sure. I'm going to break him. I just need a little more time to work on him, then he'll give us a confession." Lewis spun to look at her. "I know you two had a thing when you were younger, but he's not that man anymore. He's dangerous. Your dad and I were building a case against him, one that he wouldn't be able to slither out of like last time. His fucking brother has powerful attorneys on the case, but even they won't get him off these murder charges. He's going to get the death penalty. I promise you that."

"How…I mean…wouldn't he have covered his tracks?"

"Listen to me, Elise, that bastard isn't the same boy you knew in school. He's a cold-blooded murderer. Chang was there. The shot rang out as Chang pulled up but before he could do anything, your dad's cruiser blew up. He saw Flash there. He chose to try to save Dalton instead of going after him, so he called it in and did what he could. Flash Arquette was arrested a little while later."

"Was Officer Chang injured?" Jac inquired.

"Superficial burns. He's back to work today." He barely looked at Jac, keeping his attention on her. "The office isn't important right now. Why don't you let it go until after the funeral? I know there are a number of things to attend to right now."

"Okay." She put the picture down and focused again on the picture of her and her parents. "Actually, I think I'll take this, if you don't mind. Dad loved this picture and I can find comfort in that. It will remind me they're together."

"Go ahead." He nodded to the picture. "If you need anything, call. I'll always be here for you. Day or night."

"Thanks." She grabbed her bag and left the box sitting on the desk. "I'm just going to leave this for when I come back."

Lewis touched her shoulder and it took everything in her not to cringe or pull away. "Watch your back."

"What?" She turned enough to look at him and his fingers dug into her shoulder.

"Flash is locked up now, but it's only a matter of time before the attorneys Rocco hired get him out. As much as I try to crush their motions, we both know Rocco has connections." His gaze narrowed down on her, making her feel small under his stare. "Rocco's staying in town. I just don't want either of them to bother you."

"I doubt there's anything to worry about." *From them*, she mentally added.

"Don't underestimate them. They're dangerous. They have others working for them. I just want you to be careful. Consider who you let in and the source before you trust them."

"Don't worry, Dad taught me well." She didn't smile as she returned his gaze. It might not have been her best move but she wanted him to consider her a threat, because if he thought he could walk over her, he was about to have a rude awakening.

"Don't worry about her, she's a better shot than me." Jac came up to her other side and placed his arm around her shoulders again, forcing Lewis to remove his hand. "She's not going to be alone. As long as she's in town, so am I. You ready, babe?"

Without taking her gaze from Lewis, she nodded. "I'll see you at the service tomorrow then?"

"We'll all be there." He nodded and walked them to the door. "One more thing, Elise. If you see Craig Freeman, you might want to keep your distance from him. His drinking has made him abusive and he's barely hanging on to his job. I'm sure he'll be by to see you and I wouldn't want him to cause you more problems."

"Thanks for letting us know." Jac lead her away from Lewis, toward the exit.

If it wasn't for Jac leading the way, she wasn't sure if she'd have remembered how to get out of the police station. Her brain wouldn't focus on anything except the hatred that was growing within her for Lewis. He was trying to turn her against everyone but it wasn't going to work. She had enough evidence that made her question everything. The sudden change in Lewis only served to make her question things further.

"Babe?" Jac whispered as they strolled past a couple of officers. "Are you okay?"

She nodded, not trusting her voice. She needed to focus. Some of those surrounding them were part of Lewis's team, which meant they were part of the group responsible for killing her father. Yet, she couldn't take anything in, until a flash of orange caught her attention.

She stopped in her tracks, frozen in place as her gaze locked onto Flash. The bright orange jumpsuit pulled tight over his broad chest, his thick muscled arms straining the thin fabric to its limits. Tattoos ran up both arms and even from a distance, she could tell he'd added to them since the last time she'd seen him. Did he still have the one they'd designed together? Or had he wanted to put the past behind him and covered it over?

Needing to take him in completely, she let her gaze travel over his body before finally moving to his face. She put off looking him in the eye because his gaze always made her feel as if he knew what she was thinking. Maybe he did;

maybe that was why he had always been there when she needed him. In the past, she might have cherished that connection but right then, she didn't want him to mistake the pain and anger within her to be because of him.

Standing before her in the jailhouse uniform, handcuffed and shackled, he looked as dangerous as Lewis believed. The rest of Pinewood might think the worst of him and they might have already decided he was guilty, but she knew a different side of him. There was no mistaking Flash could be dangerous if the situation required it, but with her, he'd always shown a softer side. She'd never felt as loved, protected, and cared for as she had in his arms.

His gaze narrowed in on her, and unlike when he normally looked at her, there was no sparkle in his eyes from the smile on his face. Now there was only darkness and the only way she could describe it was rage. He didn't appear to just be angry he was locked up for a crime he didn't commit; he seemed angry at her. Did he think she was responsible for what was happening to him? That they were working him hard because she'd pressed for them to get a confession.

The blood that dripped from his broken lip and the black eye forming made her want to know what was happening to him. The black eye might have been from his arrest, but it was obvious that the broken lip and fresh blood were due to something that had just happened. She knew what it was like when a brother in arms went down in the line of duty. The hatred and anger was overwhelming. The emotion urged everyone to do their job without mistake to bring the bastard to justice, but Flash was innocent.

In that moment, she wanted to drop all the evidence she'd gathered and demand they release him. It didn't matter that the relationship she'd once had with Flash was over and nothing could change that they now stood on different sides of the law. He didn't deserve what was happening to him. The longer he was in jail with the charges hanging over his head, the more convinced the town residents would become that he'd killed Chief Dalton. Even if the charges were dropped and someone else was arrested, he'd always be guilty in their eyes.

"We've got to go." Jac's voice came through in her ear, reminding her a lot depended on her keeping it together.

The officers were already moving Flash forward, but his gaze remained on her. So she did the only thing she could. She mouthed, I'm sorry. She *was* sorry for so much, but she couldn't explain any of it then. Maybe there'd be a chance once this was over for her to apologize, but she doubted it. *Our time has passed.*

Her attention stayed on him until the officers escorting him forced Flash through another door. Only then did she allow Jac to lead her out of the police department and back to her car. "Can you drive? I need…" She didn't know what she needed, but she was certain she was in no shape to drive.

He helped her into the passenger side, before taking the keys from her and going around to the driver's side. Moments later, they were on their way back to her place and he glanced over at her. "You realize Lewis arranged for them to bring Arquette out as we were leaving, right? He was watching to see how you'd react."

"Shit!" She hadn't thought about that. If she were honest with herself, she hadn't even considered that Lewis, Chang, or anyone else might be watching her. She had been so wrapped up in the moment. It had been the first time she'd seen Flash face to face in more than three years. Time had changed him; he was harder now, but not only that, he had bulked up. He appeared dangerous, reminding her once again that he had made the choices in his life to lead him down a different path. Leaving them facing each other from different sides of the law.

"It's fine. You did fine. Actually, better than I would have thought." He pulled out of the parking lot and back onto Pinewood Pike. "You kept it together. You didn't allow that move to distract you."

Jac's words registered, but she didn't know what to say. The only thing she could focus on was Flash. She could see him staring at her, anger in his eyes, and it broke her heart. *I'm sorry, Flash. I wish I could fix this.*

The hard bunk creaked under Flash's weight, protesting every move he made. He didn't care if the fucking thing collapsed onto the floor, as long as he could lie down. After his prison release, he hoped to never see the inside of a jailhouse again. Though he suspected that might be next to impossible now, especially in this town. He sure as fuck had never thought about murder, especially not Chief Dalton's murder.

He and Dalton might have never seen eye to eye, though it was more like Dalton hated him. But, none of that mattered to Flash. The one that mattered was El. He'd never hurt her like this; yet, when he saw her moments ago, the pain in her eyes as she looked at him was unmistakable. On the verge of tears, she stared at him. Did she believe the lies Lewis was spewing? Did she believe he was responsible for the murder of her father?

He swore that, when her lips moved, she'd mouthed she was sorry. It didn't make any sense. What did she have to be sorry for? He was the one who should be apologizing. He had hurt her so many times in the past, but this time was worse than anything he'd done before. While he might not have killed her father, he wasn't there comforting her like he wanted to be, all because of hatred.

Since his arrest, he had been trying to tough it out until Rocco got clearance for him to reveal his whereabouts. He was innocent and had an alibi, but he couldn't give it to them. So, he gave them nothing. Had his silence hurt El further? It was killing him that he didn't know what she knew or what she didn't. He wanted to speak to her, but even if she visited him in jail, everything he'd say to her would be overheard, so he couldn't give her the message he needed.

The message he had given the attorneys Rocco had hired was his only hope of warning her. She was in danger. His brother would go to her and warn her, but it wasn't the same as him being out there to protect her himself. El was stubborn and he wasn't sure if she would even listen to Rocco. If she thought he was guilty, she wouldn't heed the warning.

Lying there doing nothing was killing him, but what choice did he have? If he went about this the wrong way and told Lewis of his alibi before he had clearance, they might not back up his story. These weren't people to be fucked with. They could simply deny his claims or, if they wanted to truly fuck him over, they could delete the proof he had been where he'd been. This wasn't a simple misdemeanor; he was looking at serious prison time, and from what his lawyer told him, the district attorney would be pressing for the death penalty. He'd be sent upstate to prison, most likely to the death row cell block. Then he'd be no use to El.

"What does it matter? I've been dying a slow death for years now," he mumbled to himself as the sound footsteps neared his cage. He didn't have to open his eyes to know that the hard-soled boots making the sound would be a guard.

"The nurse will be around in ten minutes to patch you up from your fight." Something clanged against the bar. "You've been here before; you know fighting only gets you additional time. Inmates fighting only make our job harder."

And we wouldn't want to make your life harder. Flash forced himself to open his eyes, to see what jackass was believing these stupid lies. He didn't recognize the young police officer, but his dark hair and build reminded him of the man with El earlier.

Reminded him of the very moment he had been trying to forget since they'd dropped him in his cell.

His hand curled into a fist as images of the man with his arm around her flashed into his thoughts. Who was that bastard? Was she seeing someone? He shouldn't care, she was no longer his girl, but the love they'd shared still burned within him. The idea of her with someone else was enough to send him into a rage. It should be him with her, his arm comforting her as she grieved for her father. Instead, he was behind bars because some asshole had it in for him.

If he got out of this mess, there were a number of things that needed his attention. First—seeing El. He needed to see her again, maybe for his own selfishness, but he also needed her to know he was innocent. Afterwards, he'd see that Lewis paid for every punch he'd swung and every drop of blood he'd spilled.

It went against every ounce of him not to fight back against Lewis, but he chose not to because that would no doubt add additional charges. If he had wanted to, even being handcuffed to the table wouldn't have stopped him from taking Lewis down. That fucking bastard was going to pay, but first he had to get to El. Keeping El at the forefront of his thoughts would keep his anger from overwhelming him and pushing him to do something stupid.

El was the only thing that mattered. He had to keep her safe and the only way for him to do that behind bars was to keep Lewis focused on him, instead of going after her. Just a little longer and Rocco would come through, then he could protect her in person. She'll be stuck with him whether she liked it or not.

Don't let me down, Rocco.

Chapter Five

By the time they arrived back at her father's house, Elise had reined in her thoughts concerning Flash and was ready to focus on what they could accomplish to get him out of jail. Whatever Rocco thought he could achieve in the twelve hours he'd asked for, he obviously hadn't managed, otherwise her trip to the station would have gone very differently.

"When you get out, forget about the spy in the house across the street. Don't let on that you suspect someone is there." Jac pulled the keys from the ignition. "Williams is around here somewhere. He'll alert us if there's anything coming our way."

She reached over and hit the button on the garage door opener that she had remembered to grab on her way out of the house earlier. "Pull into the garage and we won't have to worry about it. Just leave enough room that you don't bang the door off the truck. Dad would ki…" Her words trailed off.

"We're going to find out what happened and get whoever's responsible." Jac pulled into the garage, killed the engine, and hit the button to close the door behind them before turning to her. "You're too close to this case—"

"It's not a case; it's my father." The anger in her voice wasn't meant for him but unfortunately, he was an easy target or actually, the only possible target at the moment. "I'm sorry, Jac. I just…"

"Don't apologize. I get it." He reached over and took her hand. "A year before you joined the team, we were called in on a case in Indiana. Multiple murders with different methods of execution. The police department was stumped. Everything they gathered pointed at multiple subjects, but the victims were identical. It was a case that got under your skin and wouldn't let you forget it, but two days after we arrived, it became personal. Williams sent me to the morgue while the rest of the team continued to canvass the area where the victim was found. We didn't have an ID on the latest victim until I arrived at the morgue."

"I remember that. They were brothers; they started to work together but it became a competition between them. The women were college aged students, all with long blonde hair, athletes. None of them should have been easy targets. Wasn't one abducted outside the gym after a basketball game?"

"That was my cousin." Jac took his hand away from hers and fiddled with the keys. "She was the one in the morgue when I arrived, her image displayed on the computer screen; otherwise I'd have never recognized her. The beating she took before they killed her was unimaginable, but because of her we were able to find them and stop them before another woman was killed. She fought back and the evidence was enough to bring them down. Once arrested, the younger brother rolled on the other one, hoping to shave off some of the prison sentence."

"I'm sorry. I didn't know."

"It's not something I discuss and with the different last names it's not something most would connect. I'm telling you this because I understand what you're going through. You want justice for your father, but you're emotionally vested in this. Williams had tried to have me removed from that case, just as he wanted to remove you from this one. I fought hard to keep you on this, but if you can't handle it, there's no shame in admitting it."

She stared past him, out the driver's side window at her father's truck. What seemed like minutes but in reality was only seconds ticked by before she shook her head. "No, I can do this."

"If that changes, you need to tell me." He reached for the door handle but stopped when he noticed she hadn't moved.

"When Rocco and then Craig came to me with their information, I wasn't sure I believed them. I dug into it because I had to eliminate any doubt." Her gaze traveled from the truck to Jac. "You probably already know or at least gathered from the conversation with Lewis that I have history with Flash. I could say I only looked into it to make sure my father had justice but then I'd be lying. I needed to know if there was a chance Flash was innocent."

"Are you prepared for the possibility that he's guilty?"

Her stomach sank at the thought but she nodded. "If he's behind this, then I want him to pay. If he's not, then I want the responsible party to be the one in prison. There's more to this. There are the questions in the autopsy you mentioned. I need to look at the reports Williams gave me to see what else they contain that's alarming. There's also this situation with Lewis and who knows who else from the department. No matter what happened with my father, Lewis needs to be brought down. Besides the prostitution ring investigation, he threatened to kill Craig if he told anyone about what happened when they arrested Flash."

"I'm going to need to speak with him so we can get his official statement. The sooner the better and I can get it to Williams."

"He's here." Preparing to get out of the car, she grabbed her bag from the floor and brought it into her lap. "He was too drunk to leave last night and was still sleeping it off when I left. I placed a note next to his keys, asking him to stay. So, he should still be here. You can speak with him and I'm going to read through what Williams gave me."

"You know him better than anyone, so you might be able to spot other abnormalities in the report. The one that stood out to me was the height. Chief Dalton was taller than me and I'm six one, yet in there it says five foot eleven." He opened the door and stepped out of the car before opening the backdoor and grabbing his go-bag from the backseat. Just like hers; she knew inside the duffle bag would be everything he needed for the next few days.

Following his lead, she got out of the car but paused as she shut the door and looked at him over the roof. "Do you think he's still alive?"

"I can see the hope in your eyes and my training wants me to tell you that there's a possibility so don't lose hope but…" He walked toward the front of the car and waited for her to join him.

"I know how it works and I know the likelihood he's alive is slim, especially considering my father. He'd have called or done something to let me know he's alive." She shrugged her shoulders, unsure why she had even asked. "There are just so many things that don't add up."

"We're working on putting the pieces together, but it's going to take time." He reached out to touch her before stopping himself. "Over the last few years we've gotten close, so I know how much your dad means to you. We'll find out what happened to him."

As they made their way inside, she considered how she and Jac had made it to the place they were at. They shared a close friendship without the strain of sexual tension. She had been there when he was going through his divorce and now he was there for her as she dealt with her situation. It was comforting to know there was someone she could count on. He had her back not only in the field but also in her life.

"Where have you been?" Craig shot up from the kitchen table when she stepped into the kitchen. "Tell me you didn't confront Lew…"

"Craig, this is Jac Armiger. He's…" Placing her bag on the counter she debated which story to tell Craig: the truth or the one she'd told Lewis. Before she could decide Jac made the decision.

"Elise and I work together. I'm here to help." He sat his bag next to the china cabinet and strolled toward the table. "We've been to the station and spoke with Lewis. He's sticking to the story that Arquette is responsible for

Chief Dalton's murder, but we've been gathering other information."

"Work together, as in the FBI? The FBI is here? Lewis knows this?" The questions blurred together and Craig's eyes grew wide.

"He thinks I'm engaged to Jac and that's why he's here. That's all he knows." She grabbed the pot of coffee and poured some for her and Jac. Stirring two sugars into Jac's mug, she didn't bother to glance over at the two men. "I'll let Jac fill you in on what he can and he's going to take your official statement on what happened during the arrest."

"Official statement? The FBI is taking over Chief Dalton's murder investigation? What happened to the state police?"

"Lewis has paid them off." Jac explained as she sat the mug down in front of him. "The FBI has been watching Lewis for some time now and with this development and Elise's involvement, our team has come in to assist. For now, you'll only see me but there are others around."

"I'll let you two handle this. I'll be in Dad's office, first door on the right in the hall, if you need me." She grabbed her bag off the counter and her coffee before leaving them to figure things out. The flash drive in her pocket was weighing on her mind and she couldn't put it off any longer.

There were answers to all the questions she had; she just had to find them.

Time to dig past the surface layer and find the truth.

She only hoped she could handle whatever she found.

Elise couldn't remember when she'd gone from her father's desk to the chaise lounge that her mother had added into the otherwise manly office, but it seemed like hours had passed. It had been the middle of the afternoon. Now only darkness could be seen outside, and the house was quiet. She leaned back, letting her head rest against the pillow; something woke her but she wasn't sure what. Letting full awareness come back to her, she ran her hand down the soft fabric of the chaise lounge.

Her mother had passed away eleven years earlier, but the chaise lounge remained in the office—another thing Dad had been sentimental about. He claimed he couldn't remove it because he could still picture her mother lounging there with one of the many romance novels she'd loved to read. That was their space; he'd work and she'd read, each doing their own thing, but still together. Now they were both gone.

Faint vibrations pulled her thoughts back to reality. Her cell phone. She sat up, searching for the phone. When she finally found it, she didn't even check the display to see who was calling before she brought it to her ear. "Special Agent Dalton."

"You better watch your step."

"Excuse me?" She didn't need to ask who it was; she knew the moment he spoke that it was Lewis.

"You brought another agent into town and I know Craig Freeman is there with you. Do you really think you'll find anything?" He didn't give her enough time to answer before questioning her again. "You had to know I'd look into his story, so why didn't you tell me you worked together?"

"I wasn't trying to hide it. I figured you knew. Jac has been in town with me before." She focused on that, hoping to get Lewis' attention away from Craig. She suspected Lewis was responsible for at least one murder, if not more; the last thing she wanted to do was put Craig in his sights. "It was an oversight and under the circumstances I'd think you'd understand it. I don't understand why you're upset."

"Are you two even engaged? Fuck it, I want him gone," Lewis nearly screamed at her.

"In a few days, he will be." She glanced up to see Jac standing in the doorway, phone to his ear, and he made a circle motion with his finger telling her to keep him talking. "Tomorrow's Dad's service and the funeral the following day. After that, he's leaving. He's got to get back to work. I've taken off a couple of extra days to deal with things here. What's going on, Lewis? You've been like an uncle to me and this hatred seems out of place. We're all angry over losing my dad, but I'm not the one you should be taking it out on."

"Don't worry, that fucking bastard got a dose of what he deserves and he'll get more when they shove the needle into his arm. *If* he lives that long…"

"The bastard who killed my dad deserves to die. I can't feel sympathy for him, no matter what he used to mean to me." She hoped he would think she meant Flash, but in her heart, she was talking about Lewis. She wasn't sure how she was going to prove it but she believed Lewis and possibly Chang were responsible for what had happened. Flash had nothing to do with it.

"Good, then stay out of my business, and I won't have to deal with you, too."

There was something about the way he spoke—the coldness in his voice—that sent chills down her spine, but before she could respond, the call ended. She sat there holding the phone, her thoughts racing. *Deal with you, too.* Did he just admit that he'd killed her father? *Dose of what he deserves.* Flash? She wanted to go to the station and find out if Flash was okay, but it would raise too much suspicion. He was in jail for killing her father; she couldn't visit him.

"Lewis called from his office at the station. There's another team watching the station; they've got pictures of him behind his desk while he was on the phone with you. The bug in his office allowed them to catch the whole thing on recording." Jac clipped his cell phone onto his jeans. "We're getting close."

"Close." She dropped her cell onto the chaise lounge and when she looked back up at Jac, she realized Craig had joined them. "Close isn't good enough."

"Elise—"

"No." She cut Jac off before he could tell her things like this took time. Time she didn't have; time Flash might not have. "There's an innocent man behind bars and Lewis's guys are attacking him."

"Williams is looking into that. It might be a break for us."

"Looking into it? Officers attacking prisoners? What the fuck is going on with this town?" Craig raged.

"Jac's right; it might be a break for us." She crossed her arms over her chest and used her hands to rub away the goosebumps. "I don't want Flash there anymore than you do, Craig, but if we can get them on camera, we'll have something to work with."

"So what, we just leave Flash behind bars and allow Lewis and who knows who else to attack him? Attacking a cop will add more charges. Those aren't charges we can do anything about. He'll go to prison all because Lewis is an asshole." Craig balled his fists. "You might be able to sit around and let justice take its course but I can't. I've got to do something."

She jumped up and went to him before he could make it down the hallway. Stopping him, she wrapped her hand around his bicep. "We're all upset, and I want him out of there as much as you do, but what are you going to do? You go up against Lewis right now and you'll be asking for trouble. Dad tried to do the right thing, gather the evidence that the FBI wanted on Lewis, and look where that got him. I don't know how he knew, or even who Dad's contact was, but I'm going to find out. This isn't just about freeing Flash or getting justice for my dad. It's bigger than that now. It's about taking down Lewis and the other dirty cops. It's about the women he's forced into prostitution and all the other horrible shit he's let happen."

"I can't sit here and do nothing."

She nodded, knowing how he felt. The worst part of police work was waiting. "I know, but you're not. You did something when you came to me. Without your statement, we wouldn't be here. Rocco wasn't enough to convince me. Especially not when he's hiding things from me. But you, Craig—I know you. You wouldn't lie about this. We're going to get through this; you have to trust me and my team to get the job done."

He stood there for a moment, making her wonder if he was going to walk out the door and blow everything. "Okay, so now what?"

"First, if my days are adding up, you have a shift at the firehouse tomorrow. You need to call off. I need you with me. The service is going to be hard enough without having to deal with Lewis. More than that, he knows you're here, which means you could be in danger." She glanced at Jac. "Back me up on this."

"No need, we already had that conversation." Jac glanced at Craig.

"He already mentioned Lewis's spy across the street, so I called and got someone to cover my shift tomorrow."

"Good." She wasn't surprised Jac had already thought of it. That was one of the reasons why they worked well together—they could predict each other's moves. "I need to call Rocco and find out if he's been able to make any kind of headway there. Then I'll fix us something to eat and we can get back to work. One thing we all know is Flash didn't kill my father. There's plenty of evidence proving the truth. The question is, who did?"

"Dinner's already taken care of. Craig made lasagna."

"Since you were still up at five this morning when I went from the living room floor to the guest bedroom, I told Jac not to wake you, but I'll reheat some for you now." Before she could argue, Craig headed down the hall toward the kitchen.

"I'll check with Mel and the team at the station and see if there's any word on Arquette's injuries." Jac strolled from the office, leaving her alone.

From the sympathy in Jac's eyes when he looked at her, she figured he knew the feelings she had for Flash weren't as in the past as she tried to tell everyone. That was just another thing they connected on. He was still in love with his ex-wife, but the woman had come to a point where she couldn't put up with his career any longer. Everyone has a moment in their life when they realize there was one person who just completed them. Jac had that with his wife, and for her it had always been Flash. They were worlds apart now, but this didn't stop the feelings from being there as strong as they had been when she'd realized it all at eighteen. *Not even different sides of the law can stop true love.*

Chapter Six

With each new development, Elise became more uncertain but the news that Rocco had just delivered seemed to transport her to a whole new world. What he was saying seemed too unrealistic to be possible but then again, that type of explanation always seemed to be the most likely option. Still, she wanted to question it, to check her searches to see if it was possible.

"Elise, did you hear me?"

Looking back up at Rocco, she once again thought he didn't fit the picture. The tailored black suit with his starched white French-cuff dress shirt made him seem like a businessman. On the surface he was, but there was more to his business than she'd ever expected. She'd never inquired as to what his line of business was, but she knew he'd made millions since opening his firm. Firm—that would bring to mind an accountant or lawyer, but now she'd just found out he actually owned a security company, Phantom Security, which hired a specialized team that led dangerous missions. The headhunters could be hired by anyone with the right amount of money, and the government often used them when they needed to catch a predator.

"Elise?"

"Sorry, Rocco." She leaned forward, placing her elbows on her father's desk. "I'm shocked. I mean, I knew you were in business, but I never considered what you did."

"Most of it is legal and nothing to worry about. The main aspect of

Phantom Security is to provide protection to those who need it. Even some of what we've done for the government is on the up and up. We've transported witnesses for witness protection, protected those who needed it when their trial was coming up, and so on."

"Whatever you were doing when my father was murdered wasn't legal, obviously, or there wouldn't be so much red tape and Flash wouldn't still be in jail. So why are you telling me this? You said it yourself the other night the information you already gave me was more than I should know, placing us both in danger."

"Do you know I wanted to recruit you?"

"What?" It was hard enough wrapping her head around his news, let alone this newest information.

"Flash forbade it. He didn't want you in danger, and he knew your father would have had a fit if he found out. Your dad was never fond of the Arquette family." He clasped his hands in front of his waist and watched her. "My company was never off the record; you can search online and see for yourself. The rest of this is such, though, and I'm only telling you any of it now because it's why Flash has found himself in this situation."

"Then tell me everything. I don't have time to beat around the bush with you. I have to be at the funeral home in an hour."

"Assistant Director Winstead hired my company to infiltrate Lewis' organization." He leaned forward and held out his phone to her. "I believe you've seen this picture already."

She stared down at the same image Williams had showed her in the back of the van. Only this image wasn't as grainy as the one he had. Now she could clearly make out Lewis standing over a dead woman, blood everywhere, including on his hands. "How did you get this?"

"Scan forward; you'll see additional images." When she hesitated, he nodded toward the phone. "Go ahead, there's nothing you haven't seen before.

She was one of mine and Lewis killed her. He didn't know who she was, but when they put her through their medical tests, they found out she was a diabetic. It was under control with insulin but they didn't want to deal with it, so instead of letting her go, Lewis slit her throat. There was nothing any of us could do. The team was close by, but there was no warning. He just came in and slit her throat. If we had taken him down then, we wouldn't have gotten the rest of the information."

"The rest?" She sat the phone on the edge of the desk, closer to him.

"A second girl was part of the sting. The handoff went down; she got information on Lewis and some of the team, including Chang. The pimp she was handed off to was arrested the next morning on unrelated charges, so Lewis wouldn't get wind of it. It allowed us to free our girl."

"I still don't understand. How is Flash tied to this?"

"Do you remember Lexi? If not, there's a picture in my phone of her." He reached for the phone.

"No, I remember her. She was a year or two younger than me, but her brother…" A ball dropped into place and she was starting to catch up. "Her brother was part of the motorcycle gang Flash ran with until Flash spent two years in prison. When he came out, the gang broke up; most of the guys were in prison on drug charges. What does she have to do with this?"

"Four months ago, Flash was arrested on kidnapping charges in New York. Before anything could come of it, the FBI swooped in with a deal. Lexi had gone missing almost a year before Flash found her. Some people thought she'd skipped town but her parents knew it was something more. She was one of the girls Lewis had turned into a whore." Rocco rose from the chair and paced the small office. "Flash was in the city because of me. We were supposed to have dinner but I cut out early because of a situation with one of the teams. He hung around in case I got free but I didn't. While driving around the city, he spotted Lexi on the corner. She was high as a kite. He noticed the pimp and some of other guys in the area so he acted like he wanted to buy her services. She got onto the bike and he took off with her. He wanted to get her away from the situation and get her clean. He knew she wasn't hooking out of her own willing, but was forced into that situation by Lewis and his men. Flash was there when we interviewed her co-worker, who swore it was Chang who'd forced Lexi into the back of his car the night she went missing. Seeing her made him not only want to save her but he thought she could help expose what was happening in Pinewood. Except her pimp claimed to be her boyfriend and filed a missing person's report. He didn't want to lose the income she brought him. That's why Flash was arrested when she was spotted with him. She was too strung out and terrified of her pimp to clear him."

"Wait, I ran Flash's record. The only thing after his prison stint was a drunk and disorderly charge my dad booked him with eight months ago. He was drunk and got into a bar fight." She remembered that charge as clearly as she remembered her own name because of the length of time since he got into trouble. Eight months was a lifetime for him.

"Assistant Director Winstead knew Flash didn't kidnap Lexi so she offered him a deal. Flash would work with my team to bring Lewis down and in exchange, they'd make the charges disappear. Flash was a local; he wouldn't cause suspicion if he kept an eye on what was happening in town. He'd alert us when a girl went missing, what Lewis was up to, and anything else he found. He was part of the team that followed the two women Lewis took that were ours. That's why he was in New York the other day. We were debriefing Assistant Director Winstead."

"Then where is Assistant Director Winstead? Why hasn't she come forward and alibied Flash? Why hasn't she taken down Lewis? What the hell are you people doing?" Anger seeped from her as she eyed Rocco. "My team has gathered enough evidence in two days to take Lewis down. We've been able to trace seven women directly to Lewis. He hasn't covered his tracks well."

"A plan was set." He placed his hands on the back of the chair that he had been sitting in minutes before.

"What stopped you? Why is he allowed to continue to walk free when I'm about to put my father in the ground?" But was she? Was it really her father? If it wasn't, who was it?

"I made the call." His fingers whitened as he gripped the chair. "No one on the team had access to this information, including Flash, but Chief Dalton was working with Assistant Director Winstead, too. After I learned Flash was arrested for your father's murder, I considered the possibility Lewis was responsible. I've had my team working to gather evidence. Elise, I wanted to bring him down for everything, not just for the prostitution, but Chief Dalton's murder as well."

"So what now?"

"We have enough to take him down—maybe not enough for murder charges to stick, but we could make it happen now. It would get Flash released but it might not give you the justice you deserve." He let go of the chair and shook his head. "If we're going to do that I'm going to need to meet with your boss. Someone from the FBI needs to lead this."

"What about Assistant Director Winstead?"

"She's not returning my calls. I don't know where she is. Hell, I'm telling you all this without proper authorization. This is why I haven't been able to get Flash out yet. She's disappeared. I'm getting the run around from all my contacts at the FBI." He snatched his phone off the desk and pressed a few buttons before looking back up at her. "Everything we've gathered is now in your email. I'll meet with your boss to debrief him if necessary and my men are standing by if they can be of any assistance. Without Assistant Director Winstead, we lack the authority to proceed. I'll let you know if I'm able to get in touch with her or if we can garner any new information, otherwise you have my number if you need anything. For what it's worth, I'm truly sorry about Chief Dalton. He might not have cared for the Arquette family, but I know he was a good man."

"Wait." She stopped him before he could leave the office. "It was a breach of protocol telling me everything you did, but thank you. Lewis has been like an uncle to me, I never would have thought he would be capable of any of this, especially not killing my father. I want to see him pay for everything he's done but there's more at work here than just what I want. Women are being drugged and forced into prostitution by him and that has to be stopped. As much as it pains me to say it, we have to bring him down."

"Whatever you need from me."

"Good." She scooted the chair back and came around to stand near him. "I'm too close to the situation and I don't want to cost us the case because we moved too early. I'm going to ask you to brief Jac Armiger—he's here posing as my fiancé—and I'll get my boss Supervisory Special Agent Williams on the phone so you can speak to both of them at once. They'll know when we're ready."

He nodded but didn't say anything. She started to walk past him but then stopped again and reached out to place her hand on his arm. "You have always tried to protect Flash, first from your father, then from life, but he made his own choices. No matter what he's done in the past, it won't affect the here and now. We have enough evidence to prove he's innocent and we'll get him out of this."

"His past doesn't affect the here and now." He shook his head. "Bullshit. You still love him and I know he's never stopped loving you."

"Our time has passed." She squeezed his arm and walked to the door. They had less than an hour before she needed to be at the funeral home and she was planning a mission to take down Deputy Chief Lewis. It was insanity, but such was her life. At least she knew that her father would understand. *I'm doing this for you, Dad.*

Both emotionally and physically drained, Elise dropped down onto the sofa. If she had realized how much all of this would have taken out of her, she might have considered combining the viewing and funeral into one day. It was too late now to change things and with the viewing over, all she had to do was get through the funeral the next day.

"You okay?" Jac leaned against the doorframe, watching her as he popped open a beer.

"Just tired."

"You know, there's no shame in admitting you're not okay." He took a swig from the beer bottle before coming toward her.

"This morning we were planning a takedown and I had hopes that my father's murderer would actually end up in prison. Now I sit here…" She wasn't sure how to put what was running through her thoughts into words.

"What?" He came around the sofa and set his beer bottle on the coffee table so that he could remove his suit jacket.

"That's not my father in the casket." Without looking away from him, she slipped her heels off. They had worked together long enough to know if he was holding something back and just like she suspected, his eye twitched, giving him away. "Were you even going to tell me or were you planning on letting me continue to grieve for my father? Is he even dead?"

"Elise…" He tossed the suit jacket over the arm of the sofa and sat down next to her. "We don't know anything for certain. There are a few pieces of information Williams has found and I just learned about this an hour ago. It wasn't something we could discuss in public and once we were back here, I wasn't sure how to tell you. If we're wrong and I give you false hope, you can't rebury him."

"Just tell me." Against the funeral director's wishes, she'd opened the casket before anyone could arrive for the viewing. Even though it wouldn't be open during the service, she had to see. She'd hoped that looking at the body inside would prove it wasn't her father. Rather than knowing this without a doubt, all she could see was a victim who had been burned to a crisp. It was impossible for her to make out any of his features, so she couldn't tell.

"The blood type is different."

The information was sinking in and anger grew within her, only she didn't know who she should direct her rage at. It wasn't Jac's fault. Did Lewis do this? Did he know the murdered victim wasn't her father?

The doorbell rang and Jac got up off the sofa. "I'll get it."

"Wait, Jac." She turned to look at him. "Who is it then? I mean, if it's not my dad."

"Williams is working on it." His lips curved down into a frown. "I'm really sorry, Elise. We just don't know yet."

Didn't know? How was that possible? Whoever was killed had been in her father's police curser. There had to be some record. Had her father arrested the person? Maybe someone's vehicle broke down and he was transporting them back to town? She leaned back against the cushions and closed her eyes. None of the possibilities seemed likely, which made it likelier that the whole mess was one big set up. The question therefore remained: Where was her father?

Needing to know if there was any new information, she grabbed the small purse that held only her badge, ID, gun, and cell phone. Carrying only what was important, she'd left everything else behind in her other bag. When she slid her fingers over the smooth edge of her cell phone, a noise from the entryway caught her attention—the sound of a scuffle. Forgetting the phone, she grabbed her weapon and moved toward the archway.

As she moved into position, something broke; glass shattered as it hit the tiled floor. She could only assume the bowl her father would drop his keys into when he'd come through the door got knocked off the table. With a deep breath, she raised her weapon and prepared to go around the corner to face whoever was there.

"I'll ask you again; who the fuck are you and where is she?"

She recognized that voice but that didn't prepare her for what she faced as she came into the entryway. Flash had his hand wrapped around Jac's throat, pinning him against the wall. Jac was fighting back, but his strength was no match for Flash. Her colleague must have gone for his weapon because it now lay discarded a few feet from them.

"Let him go." Keeping her weapon steady, she focused on Flash. *Please don't let it come to this. Don't make me pull the trigger, Flash.*

"El." His grip loosened but he didn't let go of Jac as he glanced toward her.

"That's Special Agent Jac Armiger and unless you want to find yourself behind bars again, you'll let him go. Assault on an FBI agent is the last thing you need."

"You're okay? He didn't hurt you?" Flash dropped his hand away from Jac's neck and stepped back.

"Jac, you okay?" She didn't take her eyes off Flash.

"I'm fine." He retrieved his gun and slipped it back into the holster. "What the hell was that about?"

Footsteps were coming up the stone walkway and with the door still partially opened, she had a split-second choice to make. Keep her attention on Flash and hope that whoever was coming through the door wasn't a threat, or adjust her weapon and hope Flash wasn't the factor she had to worry about. Going with her gut, she aimed her gun at the door.

"Fuck, Flash, I told you to wait." Rocco pushed the door open, but stopped in the doorway when he realized she had a gun pointed at him. "What the hell, Elise?"

"Why don't you tell me?"

"El…" Flash stepped between her and Rocco. "Look at me. It's my fault, he had nothing to do with this just now. You want to shoot someone, then let it be me."

"You're out." She wasn't sure why she even said that because obviously, he was out or he wouldn't be standing in her house. In the distance, she could hear the ring of a phone but it barely phased her. "How?"

"I just picked him up," Rocco explained.

"Get in here and shut the door. Now!" Jac ordered. "Elise—"

Whatever he was going to say was drowned out by chaos. Gunshots echoed in the space around her and the glass window next to the door exploded, sending fragments through the air. Flash grabbed her, taking her to the floor in one quick action. Crouching over her, he forced her farther away from the door.

"Mick is coming," Jac told her as he kept low and moved into the living room.

She wasn't going to follow him. Going in there might give them a place to take cover and return fire, but more damage would be done if they waited the attackers out. Whoever was shooting at her house obviously wanted her or all of them dead. It was likely they'd come in to ensure the job was done. Then, she'd have her chance.

"Rocco?"

"I'm here," he whispered, coming up on the other side of Flash, gun in hand. "What's the plan?"

"We move to the office." Jac squatted near them. "This place is about to get hot. Molotov cocktail. Now, let's move."

Looking past him, she could see the first flicker of flames and that was her final straw. "No."

"What?" Flash wrapped his hand around her bicep.

"He's taken enough from me already. He's not doing this. Not here. Not now." She tugged her arm free and moved out of his reach.

"Stand down," Jac ordered. "Mick is on his way and Williams isn't too far behind. Once we have backup—"

"Screw backup. Williams can fire me if he wants, but this is my home. These are my memories…" She'd face the consequences when they happened, but now she was going to take the focus off the home she grew up in and bring it on her. It might be stupid but this was the place where she remembered her mother the most, as well as the only thing she had left of her father's, and she might never find out what actually happened to him.

Flash hooked his arm around her waist and pushed her back against the wall. "Memories aren't worth dying for."

"Let me go!" She held her gun in her hand, but she wouldn't use it on him.

"No." He lowered his head, bringing his mouth next to her ear. "I never thought I'd see you again, let alone touch you. Now that you're here in front of me, there's not a chance I'm letting you walk out that door to your death. I'll kill Lewis before he can lay a hand on you."

"Elise, they're here," Jac whispered, his voice cutting through the stillness of the night—and in that moment she realized the sound of gunfire had stopped.

"Tell them to hold off. The police are coming. If anyone in Lewis' pocket sees them, our hand is blown."

Jac relayed the message before turning his attention back on her. "If we're set on doing this, we're going all in. Flash, you need to exit from the back door and meet the van around back."

"What?" Still pressed up against the wall, she turned her head to look at Jac.

"He was just released and we don't have the whole story yet. Keeping him here will invite more questions. They'll consider him a prime suspect until otherwise convinced. Everything will get back to Lewis before we have…" Jac stopped himself before giving too much away.

"He knew I'd come." Flash took a step back. "El, are you sure you can trust him?"

"He just offered to go against the book and get you out the back door and you're doubting him?" The look in his eyes told her that if she had any doubt about Jac, she needed to state it then. They were putting their lives in his hands. But there was not a single ounce of doubt; she trusted Jac as much as she trusted anyone. She shook her head. "Yeah, I trust Jac. Besides, we've worked together for years and he's been here helping me get…"

"Fire's out." Rocco dropped the fire exhauster to the floor and glanced between them. "What's going on?"

Flash glanced back at Jac for a moment and then turned back to her. "Lewis knows you've been looking into what happened. Shit, El, he has the fucking house bugged. He's been listening to you since…fuck, I don't know how long but from what he said, it sounds like too long. He has someone watching you. Close. I thought it was Jac, that's why I—"

"Attacked him?" she supplied. "Well, it's not Jac. Which leaves Rocco or Craig. But you already ruled them out because you trust them, don't you?"

"Where's Craig?" Rocco asked. "He said he was coming back here."

"Shower. Someone needs to check on him." With the bullets flying, she hadn't thought about the man but he was farther away from all the action, so he should have been safe.

"El, no matter what you think about me right now or whether you think I'm a murderer or not, I'm trying to protect you. Lewis wants you dead."

Before she could respond, police swarmed through the front door. Each of them were separated and questioned. As she waited in the living room, she grabbed her purse. Slipping her gun back inside, she pulled out her cell phone. As she had no idea how long she had before the officer returned to question her, she shot Williams a quick message, hoping he'd be able to put the pieces together. *Flash is out. Lewis is watching me. Knows everything. Change tonight's plan.*

Chapter Seven

Being out of jail should have felt marvelous but Flash couldn't stop thinking that his release had set something else in motion. What was Deputy Chief Lewis's next action? If the murder of Chief Dalton couldn't be pinned on him, Lewis would want to find something else to stick, or find a way to take him out. Was that the reason for the attack on El's home minutes after he'd arrived? Was Lewis demented enough to think that would work?

Now that the police were done questioning him, he needed to find her, but the officer he'd spoken with had told him to wait there. He was never one to do what someone else told him, but he didn't want to make things harder for her. So, he waited patiently, watching as the police cars disappeared one by one. When they were all gone, he'd go to her; otherwise, if she wanted him before then, she'd find him. He was biding his time, playing through the conversation they'd have over and over in his mind.

He'd only got to tell her a piece of the situation before the cops broke them up. If Jac wasn't working with Lewis, then who was it? Not Rocco, for sure, and he'd known Craig his whole life; he didn't suspect him either. Who were Mick and Williams that Jac mentioned? How did they play into it? There were too many questions and he didn't have enough information. Rocco had started to fill him in on what had happened since his arrest, but there was too much to take in and not enough time on the drive from the station to El's.

"Mr. Arquette."

He turned from the window where he had been standing to find Jac standing there. He was surprised by the FBI agent's presence, but the blood on his white dress shirt caught his attention. "What happened? Is El okay?"

"Craig was shot. He's been taken to the hospital."

"El?" Fisting his hands, he gave the agent another chance to answer. Otherwise, he'd find out for himself.

"If you want his help, then you need to be upfront with him." Rocco came up behind Jac. "She's gone."

"What?" The word came out louder than he wanted, but anger rolled through him. "How the fuck did this happen? I thought you had someone watching the place?"

"We found the inside person, except he wasn't inside the house like you thought."

Rocco shook his head and stepped past Jac. "We'll fill you in on the road. Now, are you going to help rescue your girl or not?"

"Assistant Director Winstead cleared your weapons permit when you signed on to work with Phantom Security, so if you're ready, we'll gear up on the way. Leave the one you're carrying here. I don't need any illegal guns on this already fucked up mission. You've got two minutes, then I'm leaving." Jac turned around and headed toward the living room.

"Lewis has her?" He eyed his brother.

"Where's the gun?" Rocco watched him closely.

"Not on me. I'm not stupid. I knew I'd be searched." He grabbed his leather jacket off the edge of the bed and shrugged it on. "I'm taking your lack of an answer as a yes, so let's go."

"This is going to be personal for everyone involved. You're in love with her. Williams and Jac have worked with Elise for years but Lewis's spy is someone they've known longer. Mick joined the team five years ago and now he's betrayed them." Rocco strolled down the hall, toward the living room.

"Everyone is invested in this, which is going to keep emotions high, so you need to keep yourself in check. Unlike other missions I've brought you in on, we're not going to be surrounded by my people; we're going to be surrounded by FBI agents. If you fuck this up, it won't only cost the company the government contract, but also your freedom."

"I don't give a shit what happens to me as long as El's okay." He stepped past his brother. Every minute they wasted was another minute she'd remain in Lewis' hands. He was ready to do whatever had to be done to protect her. He had gone to great lengths to protect others in the past; he wasn't about to fail his woman now. This mission wasn't about him or anyone else, but about El. She was the only woman he could ever picture spending his life with. She was his world, his everything. Even once he'd stepped out of her life, he'd never stopped thinking about her. *I'm coming for you, El.*

To say the day hadn't gone how Elise had planned was an understatement. Since they'd left the funeral home, everything had gone to Hell. She'd reached the point where she didn't care how the day ended as long as it did. The last monumental fuck up of the day might not have been the worst but it had the possibility of being her last ever. The current predictive she found herself in could very likely end with her death and her biggest regret was not apologizing to Flash. A private moment alone with him was all she needed, but now it may well be too late.

Dizzy and groggy, she leaned back against the cold stone wall and tried to remember how she got there. Her memory was almost a blur but she could see herself on the deck back at her father's house, staring up at the stars in the sky, just like she used to do when she was a little girl. Focusing on that allowed the rest of the memory to flow forward.

You need to come with me. Jac will keep the Arquettes occupied. Williams found something he needs to show you, alone. Even now she could hear Mick's voice in her ear, repeating those very words. The way he'd stressed 'alone' had made the hairs on the back of her neck stand up but she hadn't trusted her instincts. Rather, she'd trusted him and the fact they had worked together for years. With a final glance at the house, where Flash waited, she'd followed him around the side toward the van.

"That motherfucker drugged me!" Her stomach rolled as she tried to force her body to stand. She had been in and out of consciousness but she needed to stay focused. Someone might be coming for her but she couldn't rely on that.

Luck had been on her side for a moment and before he'd brought her to the room, no one had searched her. It was unusual for him to overlook such a critical step but everything about the night's behavior was out of character for him. Once alone, she was able to shoot a quick message to Williams. *Help! Mick.* It had been only two words but without knowing when they'd be back, she couldn't take the chance of not being able to send anything. Mick returned, snatching her phone away from her and stomping it to bits before she had been able to see if the message had gone through. *I left your phone because they'd kill me if they found one on me but you can't call in the cavalry; you'll get her killed. Trust me, I'll be back for you.* Maybe it was the drugs but Mick's rant as he destroyed the phone made little sense to her. Get who killed? Trust him? How was she supposed to trust him after he kidnapped and drugged her? For now, she could only hope Williams had received it and possibly be able to determine her location before it was too late. Otherwise, with whatever drug Mick had injected her with, she was going to have a hard time getting out of this situation alive. Having no weapon, either, her ability to fight back was severely compromised.

She wasn't sure where she was but from the cold, stone wall, the only place she could think of was the old winery on the outskirts of Pinewood. Under the factory ran a tunnel that had once allowed the workers an easy way to travel to and from the staff's living quarters. She didn't know of any rooms off of it but she hadn't been there since she was a child.

The door opened and Lewis strolled toward her. She caught a glimpse of Chang outside the door before Lewis slammed it shut, drawing her attention back to him. His shirt was wrinkled as if he'd slept in it; the lines around his eyes pinched together, which was something he only did when he was worried. He was in over his head and he knew it. Her team was closing in on her and even if they didn't rescue her, they'd take him down. There was enough evidence to convict him on multiple charges—maybe not for her father's murder, but at least she could die knowing he'd be behind bars soon enough.

"I warned you to stay out of this, but you didn't listen. No, you're too much like your father. Too bad you're going to die like him." Reaching up, he let his fingers trail across the curve of her cheek. "If you'd have only listened, I could have found a use for a beautiful thing like you."

"Fuck you." She scooted down the wall, farther away from him.

"Don't you know that's what I've wanted to do since you turned eighteen? But you never looked at me like you looked at Arquette. Don't you worry, beautiful, your criminal lover is going to be dead soon, too. You can be together in death." Closing the distance, she put between them, he placed a hand on each side of her so she couldn't move away without ducking under his arms. "Then there was your father. He'd have never gone for it. I think he'd rather you were with Arquette than me. But, I took care of him. When I did, I thought you'd turn to me, seek comfort in my arms. But then this fiancé shows up out of nowhere. Tell me, beautiful, are you two actually engaged? Before you speak, know that your answer will decide if I let him live or kill him, too."

"Then, it's true, you killed my father?"

"Just like I'm going to kill you."

His words had her seeing red and in a flash, she brought her knee up, connecting with his manhood. With her hands tied together in front of her, she went for his gun and pulled it from the holster before his hand clasped over her wrists, stopping her.

"Don't even think about it, bitch." With his other hand, he reached up and backhanded her.

She wouldn't let go; she couldn't. It was her only chance. Fight or die. Those were her choices and even as the room swayed and her stomach protested every movement, she fought. Fighting over a gun could be deadly, so she tried to remain vigilant about where the muzzle was pointed. She didn't want to give him a chance to shoot her. *Focus.*

He slammed her back against the wall hard enough that her head bounced off the stone surface and her grasp on the weapon loosened. She didn't let go but he was able to readjust it. Before she could regain control, the gun went off. Pain exploded along her thigh.

"Ah!" She gritted her teeth to stop her from crying out.

"That hurts, doesn't it?" The glimmer in his eyes let her know he enjoyed seeing her in pain. "If you don't let go of it now, I'll make sure the next one isn't just a grazing wound."

"Why…tell me why you killed my father? Before you kill me, I just want to know what gave you the right to kill him. He gave you a chance after what happened in Virginia. He brought you into not only the department, but our family. You were like an uncle to me."

He was silent for so long, she thought he wasn't going to answer her but since he was no longer struggling to take the gun away, she remained still and waited. It might be dragging out her death, but she was hoping it would give her team time to save her. *Flash, you've always known when I needed you. Please, Flash, I need you now.*

"He got too close, he dug too deep, and it was either him or me. I'm not ready to die."

"Dug into what?" She had to keep him talking. The more he talked, the better the chance they'd find her.

"You still haven't figured it out yet. Maybe you're not as smart as your father bragged." He chuckled and with one swift punch to her other side, he pulled the gun out of her grip and she slid down the wall. "The incident in Virginia you mentioned, the one where I shot a kid. He never had a gun; I planted that. He caught on to what I was doing and would have caused me trouble but I killed him before he could."

"What were you doing?" Her body too spent to move, she sat there on the cold floor.

"You ask a lot of questions, but since you're going to die, I guess it doesn't matter." He took a step back and trained the gun on her. "I kidnap girls to sell. Some of them work as prostitutes, some are sold as wives, others go to the highest bidder to do what they wish with them. The money is good but it didn't start out because of that. I did it because I had to. I owed a loan shark a lot of money and he was growing impatient. He offered to forget my debt if I got a girl for him. Not any girl but the girl that kept turning him down. I didn't have a choice, but it was so easy. Now I can't give it up; the power and the high I get from it are better than any drugs in the world."

She wasn't sure what to say to his confession. Anything that came to mind would only anger him and most likely cause her more pain or her death. Unlike when she was working on a case, she couldn't detach herself from the situation. This was too personal, too deeply connected to so much of her past. For years, she'd confided in this man. He had been there for her like an uncle, especially after her mother died. To now discover this side to him disgusted her.

"I've watched you. You're so beautiful. The way you dance when you think no one is watching. The way you curled up on your bed and comforted Bear when he broke his leg. You took a week off work, used your vacation time, to care for him."

"What?" There was no way he could have known the things he was saying, yet he spoke as if he had seen it with his own eyes.

"The way the water drips off your hair and down your shoulders while you're applying lotion to your legs." He let out a soft moan. "You've been a temptation for years and the moment I think I can claim you, you do something stupid. Now you're too much of a liability, and I have to kill you."

"You've been watching me? For how long?" She pushed herself up the wall until she was leaning against it as she tried to regain her balance.

"You're catching on. Years, beautiful, years. I looked forward to your monthly visits. You've grown into a gorgeous woman."

Forgetting about the gun, she pushed herself off the wall, launching herself at him. Anger overtook her as she slammed her bound wrists into him, over and over again, aiming at whatever was available. His head, chest, arms, whatever she could hit, all the while wishing she'd grabbed a rock or had a knife. Something to do real damage.

It didn't take much for him to push her away. She grabbed onto his shirt, wanting to take him with her, and her legs gave out, sending her stumbling back to the floor. His shirt ripped, breaking her hold, but not before he ended up kneeling on the floor in front of her.

"You little bitch." He backhanded her hard enough that she could taste blood. "Seems you weren't given enough."

She tried to make sense of his words but before she could, he shoved a needle into her arm. *Fuck!* Her body was just beginning to work through the shit Mick had given her; another dose would send her back into unconsciousness. She had minutes to get away from him before she'd be helpless.

"I'm not ready to kill you yet." He grabbed hold of her arm and dragged her back up onto her feet before he leaned in close enough so his breath brushed along her cheek. "I want you to see proof your criminal lover is dead. I want you to see what I'm going to do to him. Then, when you're terrified about what I'm going to do to you…maybe then, I'll end your life, too."

The door behind them flung open with such force, it slammed into the wall, revealing Flash. "Get away from her!"

"Who's this? Oh, I see, it's the criminal bastard who murdered her father, coming to rescue her." Lewis brought his weapon up and trained it on her. "Go ahead, shoot me. Show her you're the murderer I know you are. But when you do, know it will cause her death as well."

With Lewis focused on her, he was forced to give Flash his back. Their eyes locked and as if silently communicating, she knew what he needed her to do. She flung her arms out, forcing Lewis's arm up and away from her. When his finger jerked he pulled the trigger, sending debris from the ceiling down, she rolled to the right.

Everyone always expected Flash's dominant side to be his right, but after his motorcycle accident injuring his right arm, he was stronger with his left. Being aware of this gave her an edge to know she'd more than likely be out of his way in the right corner of the room. All the stupid self-defense lessons he'd forced on her during their high school days now seemed worth it. She knew what his next move would be and all she needed to do was keep the adrenaline going enough to get out of the way before the drugs took over. Her legs were already weak and fog was settling over her brain. It wouldn't be long now before she became unconscious.

Flash charged before Lewis realized what was happening. The gun was still in his hand, but as Flash's fists connected to the side of Lewis's head, it didn't appear he'd get a chance to use it. Flash faked with his right and slammed home with his left.

"Elise." Rocco stood out of the way, near the door, beckoning her in.

Jac grabbed her arm; she hadn't even noticed him until he started to pull her to her feet. "We're going, now."

"Flash…"

"I've got this," Jac reassured her. "You go with Rocco. Williams is down the hall."

71

"Don't…don't kill him." She glanced back at the fight before looking back at Jac. "Flash…don't kill Flash."

"Why would I? He's only dishing out retaliation." He pushed her toward Rocco, who caught her before she collapsed onto the floor. "Go."

"Come on, let's get you out of here. They'll be along soon." He wrapped his arm around her waist, pressing her tight against his body to keep her upright. "Don't you worry."

Not worrying was like asking the room to stop spinning around her; it wasn't going to happen. Her legs felt like lead weights, making each step difficult. She couldn't even open her mouth to reply to his comment.

"Tanner! With me!" Rocco hollered to someone, but she couldn't see through the blurriness to determine who it was. She didn't remember anyone called Tanner, but maybe it was someone from the other FBI team, the one that had been watching the station. Rocco scooped her up into his arms, carrying her. "Don't worry, I got you."

"Where are the others?" Williams voice forced her to open her eyes again.

"They're with the subject."

"S…ir…" Her tongue felt heavy and the words wouldn't form.

"You're going to be fine, Dalton," Williams assured her. "Get her out of here. Call an ambulance."

"I've got a medic on the team. He'll treat her and we'll go from there." Rocco started moving again, but she fought against his hold. She needed to see Williams. She had to tell him to get Flash and Jac. Her vision got hazier and her eyelids were nearly closed, her eyelashes like prison bars. *Prison. Flash.* A lump rose within her chest as her gaze found someone. She thought it was Williams but it was Mick. He was on the ground, his body slouched against the wall—dead. Her mind refused to allow her time to process the sight as darkness closed in around her. Fighting it only seemed to make it worse. *Don't leave me now, Flash. I need you.*

Chapter Eight

With the cold wind blowing around him, Flash stood looking out over the field, which had at one time been used to grow grapes for wine. Even in the dim moonlight he could see still extant rows, even if the weeds had begun to take over. This place had been beautiful once, but after the bank foreclosure, it just sat there, empty. The wildlife began to expand their territory, once again coming out of the woods. Now that humans weren't there, nothing could stop them. He focused on the winery so he wouldn't think about what would happen when El woke up.

The moment his attention wavered, it went straight back to El. She might have seen the evidence he hadn't killed Chief Dalton, but that didn't mean she wanted anything to do with him. The same evidence that cleared him of murdering her father also proved he was no good for her. It would kill him, but he'd leave her to live the life she wanted—only if they talked first, though. There were things he needed to say, things that had been weighing on his mind for too long.

A soft moan had him spinning around to face her. He caressed along the top of her head, allowing his fingers to tangle in the honey brown strands. "It's okay, El, you're safe."

"Flash…"

"Yeah, sweetie, it's me." He slid his hand down so that his thumb brushed along the curve of her cheek. "I know the backseat isn't comfortable, but you need to rest. We're going to get you into a bed soon."

"You're really here…you came…for me." Her eyelids fluttered as she fought to keep them open.

"I'll always come for you." He reached further into the SUV and took her hand in his. "Always, El, always."

"We need to talk." Jac came to stand next to Flash.

"No." She tried to sit up but as she did, Flash took his hand away from her head and placed it on her shoulder.

"El, you need to lie down."

"Jac…don't…" She pushed against Flash, trying to sit, but the drugs still in her system were making her too weak. It would be moments before the drugs pulled her back under. "Don't…arr…est…"

"Shh, El." He leaned down to her and pressed his lips to her forehead. "It's going to be okay." He wanted to tell her he'd be there when she woke up, but he didn't want to lie to her. He was out of jail because of Assistant Director Winstead, but his problems weren't over. The trumped-up kidnapping charge still hung over his head, since the job wasn't complete yet. Assistant Director Winstead wanted Lewis and those working with him. Instead of delivering that, though, he'd killed Lewis. He was here with Rocco's team and the FBI but that didn't mean he wouldn't face charges for what had happened in the tunnel. If he found himself back in jail, he'd do his time. El was safe and that was what mattered. It wasn't like they had a chance together anyways. Her life was in D.C. with the FBI and his…well, he wasn't sure what life had in store for him.

"I love you, El. Always," he whispered against her hair as her body stilled and sleep reclaimed her. Placing one last kiss on the top of her head, he rose to face Jac. "Let's do this." He stepped back and held out his hands, waiting for Jac to cuff him.

"You've been on the wrong side of the law for a long time."

"I know," he snapped before gaining control over his temper. Jac meant something to El; he wanted them to be only friendly coworkers, but it was obvious there was more to it. Jac could give El what he couldn't, and he needed to accept that. "Let's not drag this out. Just take me in."

"I'm here to tell you that you're officially a free man. No charges will be forthcoming. The ones Winstead used as leverage and all others are gone. A clean slate. I'm not saying it's going to be easy, but you've got a chance to turn your life around." Jac slipped his hand into his pocket and pulled out his business card before handing it to Flash. "If you need anything, give me a call. No promises, but I'll see what I can do to help."

He took the card and stared at the man. "Lewis is dead." He'd shot and killed Lewis after beating the shit out of him; even Rocco's connections wouldn't help him get out of that.

"Killed to protect two agents." Jac nodded. "You were there officially, and the actions taken in the line of duty were justified."

Williams came around the SUV and joined them. "Your actions saved the lives of two of my agents. Because of you, Elise and Jac are alive. The FBI is showing its gratitude by giving you a new life. Don't waste it."

"Thank you." The words seemed inadequate but he didn't know what else to say.

The thought of being able to put everything behind him and start over fresh was something he'd never expected to experience. Even after he got out of prison, there was no fresh start. The residents of Pinewood would never let him forget what he'd done or who his father was. To them, he'd always be guilty and that meant if he wanted to start over, he could never return there. The idea of never returning to Pinewood was unsettling. That town wasn't home and the only one there that he cared about was Craig. But, the place was his connection to El. When she went back to Washington D.C., there was no chance he'd see her again. In the end, he'd lose El again. Nothing he could do would stop it.

Rocco stepped away from his team and came over to them. "I've spoken with a physician; the drugs will take twenty-four hours to completely come out of Elise's system. During that time, she's going to be groggy, her vision might be effected, and she's going to experience what he felt safe calling the worst hangover of her life. She needs rest so, with your permission, I'd like to take Special Agent Dalton back to my penthouse in New York. Considering Lewis's reach, it's the safest place for her."

"What about the funeral? She's going to be pissed if you try to keep her away from that." As their gazes turned to him, he realized there was something he was missing. "What?"

"Chief Dalton is alive." Williams explained. "Assistant Director Winstead has had him transported to a safe location. He was shot and his car was indeed blown up but he wasn't in it when it happened. I don't have anything more, but I'm meeting with Winstead in an hour. I'm going to find out the truth and then I'll meet you at Rocco's. Meanwhile, Jac, I want you there with her. She's a target until we know otherwise. I'll send more agents over for her protection once I have them."

"There's no need for that." Rocco tipped his head to the team gathered near the entrance. "I've got my men. I can assure you, she'll be safe."

"Very well." Williams' gaze found Flash again. "I'll have agents deal with the funeral issue and Chief Dalton's house. You'll need to keep her calm until I have further information on her father. Once I have the location, I'll see about arranging transportation for them to be reunited. If he's been taken into protective custody, it's going to require additional time. Hopefully, with Lewis's death, it will speed things along. I'll be in touch when I can."

"Let me worry about her; focus on finding Chief Dalton. Work fast. I'd hate for her to learn he's alive but his condition is so grave that he dies before she can see him." He forced himself not to look at Rocco, but the moment the agents stepped away, he was going to light a fire under his brother's ass to get him digging into it, too.

"When she wakes, she'll want this." Williams handed Flash a small black bag. "Her new work cell phone is inside, as well."

He reached in to place it on the floor in the backseat and when he turned around, Williams was already moving away with Jac. Rocco leaned against the SUV. He seemed relaxed, watching those around him but Flash could tell he had something on his mind. Rather than pressing him, Flash waited, unable to fight the compulsion of caressing along the curve of El's back. The desire to climb in the backseat and hold her in his arms pulled at him. This might be his only chance, for once she was conscious he wasn't sure where things would go with them.

"You coming?"

"Did you really believe there was a chance in hell I was going to let her out of my fucking sight again? That asshole could have fucking killed her!" His voice rose as he glanced over at his older brother.

"What matters is we saved her; actually *you* saved her. You knew where she'd be even before Williams got his trace results back." Rocco shifted his gaze from El to Flash. "I need that."

"What?" This wasn't the first time he had no clue what his brother meant, but the thought he meant he needed El made him want to pummel him.

"Not her, though I want her, too. For the team, not for me," he quickly clarified before sending Flash a cocky glance. "I want you to come work for me. Full time. Lead one of the teams. You can have your choice of missions and those under you. But, I need you."

"Why?"

"I could tell you a bunch of bullshit, but the truth is Phantom Security is becoming bigger than I can handle by myself. I need someone I trust. You can put Pinewood in your rearview mirror once and for all and have a new start. Think about it." Rocco raised his hand and beckoned for Tanner to join them. "And remember, I want Elise, too. I've respected your wishes and didn't poach her to work for me, but after this, she's proven to be just what I need. She dug into your case like a dog with a bone. She wasn't going to give up."

"Because of her father."

Rocco shook his head. "Believe what you want, but I was there. It was more than that. She still loves you. This could be your chance to be together." Tanner was drawing close, ending the conversation. "Let's roll. You're in the back with her. Tanner, you drive."

Lifting El carefully, he climbed into the backseat before resting her head on his lap. He brushed the hair away from her face so he could have a better view as he watched her sleep. On the surface, Rocco's plan sounded perfect; even if she didn't join Phantom Security, their paths would cross occasionally and as long as he kept himself clean, they wouldn't be enemies. But when he dug deeper, he found flaws in the plan. The biggest being Chief Dalton. He was alive and when he found out she was with Flash, he'd have a fit. Her relationship with her father had been one of the reasons why he'd stepped out of her life in the first place. At the time, he didn't want to be the one that ruined the father-daughter bond, and he felt the same way now, especially after she thought she'd lost her father. *My sweet El...*

Every ounce of her body ached. Her eyelids felt heavy, but it was the pounding in Elise's head that proved the worst. When she finally found the strength to open her eyes, she realized she didn't know where she was. The bedroom was dark except for a small lamp on the dresser across the room. The soft glow did little to light up the massive room, but the dark wood furniture and plush forest green down comforter were enough for her to know she wasn't anywhere she'd been before, and it wasn't a hotel, either. Leaning forward so she was arched up on her elbow, a soft moan escaped as the drummers in her head banged louder.

"El." All she could see was a figure she hadn't noticed step away from the window and out of the shadows, but she knew by his voice it was Flash. "Take it easy."

"I'm…" Her stomach started to heave from the movement and she collapsed back onto the bed. "Oh, fuck."

"I know you feel like hell but it's going to pass." Careful not to jar the mattress, he sat down on the edge of the bed next to her and took her hand in his.

"You're still here." She took him in—the bruises, split lip, and the gash along his cheek. All of those she suspected were from Lewis or his guys. *That bastard!*

"And I'm not going anywhere." He squeezed her hand.

"What happened? Where am I?" She closed her eyes for a moment, trying to figure out what was real and what was a dream. "I remember the tunnel. You came for me and when I moved out of the way, Rocco was there. Shit…Mick…I saw him."

"Rocco got you out of there while Jac and I dealt with Lewis. Do you remember Tanner? He's one of Rocco's men. He checked you out once they got you outside. Once we got you here, a doctor examined you, too. Verdict is you're going to be fine; you just need to rest until the drugs are out of your system."

"Same old Flash." She chuckled, making her head hurt worse.

"Note to self, don't make her laugh."

Looking back up at him, she wasn't surprised to find his expression blank. He always did that when he wanted to hide something or didn't want to talk about the subject. It was his way of hiding, acting as if it didn't bother him one way or the other. But she could see through it, she managed to get to the real man underneath his shell. There had been a time when she didn't have to work hard to see through him. Then he had become an open book to her, showing her pages inside that no one could ever see.

"Why?" She hadn't meant to question it aloud but the question was out now. Watching his eyes, she silently hoped he hadn't heard.

"There are many different ways to take that."

"Fine, I'll be clear. I was wondering why you're trying to hide from me again. I can see through you but you know I've been drugged, so why make me work so hard? Could you just make things easy for once and fill me in on what I've missed? How long have I been out? Where's my team? Heck, how about: where am I?"

"We're at Rocco's penthouse in New York. Jac's down the hall; last I checked, he crashed in one of the guest rooms. Williams is…well, I'm not sure where he is. I just know he's dealing with something important. It's almost seven and since the doctor said the drugs you were injected with would take twenty-four hours to get out of your system, you've got a few more hours before you can get up. So, just relax."

"Seven! The funeral." Tears welled in her eyes before she could blink them away. It wasn't her father in the casket so why did she care. Those who attended would wonder where she was, but what did it matter? Most of them she'd never see again, anyways.

"Don't worry about that." He leaned forward and brushed a strand of hair from her cheek. "El, there's something you should know, but I need you to stay still. The drugs are starting to leave your system but if you do too much, you're going to make yourself sick. Trust me when I say you don't want a repeat of that."

"A repeat?" She felt the blood rush to her cheeks. "Oh, shit, I'm sorry."

"No need, sweetie. I hated not being able to do anything for you." He shook his head and started to rise off the bed but she kept hold of his hand.

"Don't." Her hold on him was loose as her muscles felt like water; they refused to work like she wanted them to. "Tell me what's going on."

"First, answer me this." He stayed on the side of the bed, his hand holding hers, but there was suddenly distance between them. "Do you believe I killed your father? Did you believe it? I have to know."

"No." She reached up to touch his face, careful of his wounds. "We're on different sides of the law, but I never believed it, even before Craig and Rocco came to me with their proof. Maybe part of me didn't want to believe such a thing because...because of what we've shared. The other part of me knew you wouldn't have done it. That's not the person you are."

"El."

Lightly, her finger touched his lips, stopping him. "Let me finish. Rocco came to me with your message, but I was angry. I'm not sure if I even know who I was angry with, but what I do know is: it wasn't with you. I was going to investigate it but my grief delayed me. Then, when Craig showed up with your wallet and the tollbooth receipt, I dug into it."

"Rocco said you were like a dog with a bone." His thumb played over the back of her hand, teasing lightly over each knuckle. "Jac filled me in on everything, including the man you were going to bury having a different blood type than the one that's on file for your father. El, they've completely ruled out the deceased as being any relation to you. It's not possible with the blood type. They're still trying to determine who it is."

"Which leaves me with more questions than answers and the one who might be able to answer them..." She realized she hadn't asked what had happened in the room. There was an outcome that she wanted; if only Flash had rescued her, it would have happened, but Jac had been there.

"Lewis is dead. A long story, which I can fill you in on, but first you need to know Williams has found information that your father is alive. Assistant Director Winstead authorized Dalton's evac."

"No." The tears returned to her eyes and there was no blinking them away. "Don't, Flash, please don't. I can't—"

"El, sweetie. I swear to you."

"No!" Screaming, she slammed her hand on his chest. "No. He wouldn't have done that. He wouldn't have let me think he was dead. He would have called." Tears rolled down her face as she slammed her fists against his chest, over and over.

He waited until she stopped hitting him before standing up and turning around so he could sit next to her, instead of facing her. "Easy, sweetie." Doing his best not to jar her, he pulled her into his arms, holding her tight against his body.

"Why?"

"I don't know why any of this happened. Lewis must have found out he was working with the FBI and when he did, I have no doubt he wanted Dalton dead. Jac believes Dalton was meeting with his contact when the whole thing went down. That might have been why they were able to get him out and to a secure location." He tugged the comforter up and tugged it in around her. "If you want my take…"

"Tell me."

"I think Chief Dalton's contact was a two-man team. One of them is the dead man and the other was able to get him away. Maybe he's given them enough information that they needed him to testify, or maybe he was taken away because he's another law enforcement agent and you don't leave someone behind. No matter the reason, they whisked him off to safety; it's likely he has severe injuries. He's unconscious or possibly sedated. Otherwise, he'd have got in touch with you. Nothing would have stopped him, not even the FBI, because he would have known Lewis would come for you. He wouldn't want to see you like this and he sure as hell wouldn't want you thinking he was dead."

"Assistant Director Winstead…" Ignoring the pain and nausea, she adjusted so she could look up at him. "I know her, more like Dad knows her. They went to school together. Not only that, she's the one Williams reports to. She'd have known we were here. That I was here."

"Williams had a meeting with her. I had hoped we'd have heard something from him before you woke up, but he hasn't been in touch yet. I hated telling you when we only know half the story but he's confident that Chief Dalton is alive." He caressed along the curve of her back. "We're going to figure it out, I promise."

Lost in her thoughts, she clung to him. For days, she'd grieved for her father, and now she found out he might be alive. She couldn't allow herself to get too emotional about it because she didn't know anything else. His condition might be grave and she might still lose him before she even got to see him again.

"I need to see Jac. I need his phone. I have to find answers."

"I'll get him, but you need to stay in bed. The more you move around, the worse you're going to feel. The shit Mick gave you was strong, but he knew it wouldn't kill you."

"No, he wouldn't want me dead; that was Lewis's pleasure." Her fingers tightened around the blanket, squeezing the fabric like she wanted to do to Mick. "He betrayed me."

"Not defending the bastard, but you'll want to read this report." She glanced up to find Jac standing in the doorway. "I was passing and heard you talking. May I?"

"Come in." Flash started to pull away from her after she invited Jac in, but she glanced up at him.

"Stay…please." At that moment, she didn't care if she looked weak, cuddled in Flash's embrace, or what Jac thought about it. All she cared about was that he was out of jail and with her. There wasn't a place she'd rather be than in his arms.

"I'm here for as long as you want me." He slipped his arm back around her.

"Here." Jac came to the side of the bed and held out a phone to her.

"Give me the shorthand version."

"One of Lewis's men kidnapped Mick's sister. She turned nineteen two weeks ago and was going to school in New York. From the timeline I've put together, I believe after Lewis saw us at the police station he did some digging, found out who I was, and figured we were all in town. Mick's sister was the only target he could use. He threatened to kill her if Mick didn't help him. Williams received your message, but moments before that, Mick called. My phone got lost in the shuffle when people were shooting at us and it wasn't until later that I got the message. He confessed everything. His plan was to use you as a distraction, get his sister, and then get both of you out of there."

"Why didn't he tell us? Why didn't he tell me? Instead, he drugged me. I wouldn't have been any help to him." Mick had gone about it all wrong, but she understood his desire to save his sister. "What about his sister? Did someone find her?"

"Dead. She was dead before you even got there. Lewis didn't need her anymore; she served her purpose. It was one less thing he had to worry about. He was about to have you hand delivered, which is what he really wanted."

"What a complete fuckup." She ran her hand over her face. "This whole assignment was a disaster. All the evidence I've seen makes me wonder why the hell Lewis wasn't taken down before. There's plenty of evidence to convict him. You know what? Screw it. Jac, let me borrow your phone, I need to call Assistant Director Winstead and get to the bottom of this."

Flash grabbed a bag off the end table. "Williams gave me this. Your new work phone is in there."

"My new work phone." She chuckled. "I should have known Williams would have a backup."

"Is that standard policy for FBI agents to carry a spare phone?"

"Standard for Williams." She opened the bag and inside sat her gun, badge, ID, and the phone. "He always carries an extra one because his phones keep getting destroyed. Last time, it was shot; before that, the phone took a swim.

Let's just say he has bad luck with phones."

"Elise, calling Winstead might not be the best idea," Jac reasoned. "Pissing off the assistant director won't be good for your career."

"Fuck my career. We're talking about my father. I deserve some answers." Before anyone else could argue with her, she typed in the number and pressed call. *One thing you don't mess with and that's family. I'm going to get answers about Dad, if I have to tear apart the FBI database myself.*

Chapter Nine

For days, Elise had been living in a nightmare and now all she wanted were answers. Assistant Director Winstead didn't answer her call and had yet to call her back. Even Williams hadn't picked up when she called. She could feel it in her bones; something was happening, yet she was being left in the dark. Jac hadn't been able to answer many of her questions, but he'd told her what he did know. He'd look into it and see what he could find but his assignment was to guard her. With her kidnapping, the operation hadn't gone down as planned. Chang and anyone else who'd worked with Lewis were still out there posing a threat to her safety.

Being in Rocco's penthouse in downtown New York City should have put distance between her and Lewis's people, but since they had been sending some of the women to New York for prostitution, it was likely the connections were just as deep, if not deeper, here. Besides Jac's presence, Rocco had his men stationed throughout the building. Even with all the precautions, the one thing that made her feel safe was having Flash by her side. With her training, she should have been able to protect herself but her vision was still affected from the drugs. The blurriness was starting to recede but she had a hard time focusing. She couldn't rely on getting an accurate shot.

"You're beautiful when you smile." Flash's words had her looking up at him. "That's the first time I've seen you smile in…shit, I can't remember when but it's been too long."

"I was thinking about shooting Chang. Well, not so much shooting him but anyone that came after me. If Lewis's team wanted to continue things, they'd need to clean up his mess, and part of that mess is me. They don't know what Lewis told me and the best way to ensure I never have a chance to take them down is to kill me."

"You're safe here." He brought his hand across his chest to lay on top of hers.

"You're worried about it, or about something. Your body went stiff and though you're looking at me, you're not meeting my eyes. Tell me what you're thinking." She separated her fingers, allowing his to slide in-between hers, interlacing them.

"Not about your safety, not here. Because of Rocco's business, he's taken extensive security measures and those precautions are the reason we came here instead of going somewhere else. I know many of the guys who are here; they'll keep you safe."

"You say that like you're leaving." She pulled back from his embrace enough to get a better look at him. "Flash? What's going on?"

"Do you want me to?" He seemed to be frozen in spot, unmoving, as if unsure what she'd say.

"No." She kept her gaze on him until he let out the breath he had been holding and his muscles relaxed. "I don't know what's happening here—between us I mean—but I don't want you to go. It's selfish, I know, because what future is there for us? Even with the charges dropped, we're different people."

"Different sides of the law?"

"There's that." She hated to admit it but that would be an issue for them. "But there's more. You have what's important to you and—"

"That's where you're wrong. I don't." He took his hand from hers and reached up to cup the side of her face, his thumb gently brushing over her bruised cheekbone. "You're what's important to me; you've always been. I almost lost you and in that moment, I realized I don't want to spend another day without you. I love you, El."

"Flash—"

"Let me finish before you say anything." He pressed his thumb to her lips, cutting her off. "When I found out you were taken, I was coming after you one way or another. I didn't care if Jac or Rocco backed me on that. Spending the rest of my life behind bars wouldn't have mattered as long as I knew you were safe. Lewis told me he was going to kill you. He made it sound like he already had you secured, that the traitor was in the house with you, controlling you. I tried to get word to Rocco or my attorneys but they were working on getting me out of jail. When they released me, the only thing on my mind was getting to you. Maybe that's why Lewis ordered the attack on your house; maybe me coming to you set the whole thing in motion but I didn't think. I had to come to you, to protect you. It was the same when I found out you were gone."

"I knew you'd come." She lifted her shoulder in a half shrug. "I can't explain it, but I knew you'd find me. I didn't know if my message got through because Mick found me texting and smashed the phone to bits. Still, I didn't lose hope."

"Coming for you gave us something I never expected. It gave us a chance." With the arm he still had around her, he pulled her back against him, holding her close to him. "I'm a free man. My convictions and any pending charges are gone."

"What? How? Who?" She wasn't sure which question was the right one, but any of them would do. The information was nearly as overwhelming as her father being alive. She just wasn't sure what that meant for them.

"Williams and Jac gave me the information and you know me I needed the proof, so I had Rocco run a background check on me. He did the same thing he'd do with anyone he was considering for employment. Officially, it was for the actions resulting in saving two FBI agents." Placing a finger under her chin, he tipped her head back up so she was looking at him. "I never expected anything like this and if you want me to be truthful, I was convinced I'd be back in jail. Only this time it wouldn't be for a murder I didn't commit, but for killing Lewis, and I would have accepted that."

"I wouldn't have."

"El, my point is we're not on different sides. I guess you could say we're on the same side. Rocco's offered me a job with his company and I'm going to take it." He paused for a second, letting that sink in. "He has a position for you, too."

"He mentioned that you forbade him from offering it to me before." She raised an eyebrow at him. "Are you trying to hold me back?"

"I was trying to protect you. Every decision I've made has been to protect you." A knock on the door forced him to stop for a moment. "What?"

"I think you need more coffee," Rocco joked as he opened the door. "That or some sleep. Though this looks pretty cozy."

"What do you want, Rocco?" Irritation was clear in Flash's voice.

"I've been tapping my sources to determine what's happened to Chief Dalton and I have a lead." Rocco strolled farther into the room and stopped on the side of the bed, looking down at her. "How are you feeling? The drugs should be mostly out of your system."

"I'm okay. Thanks, Rocco, for everything."

"No need for that. But if you're feeling guilty, you could consider coming to work for me. I promise you there's a substantial pay raise in it." He gave her a quick smile. "If you're feeling nauseous, a headache, anything, Tanner has different things the doctor left for you."

"I've already told her. Now, what did you find out?" Flash snapped.

"I believe Chief Dalton is in the Pocono Mountains in Pennsylvania. I received information that led me to investigate further. When I did, I found

Assistant Director Winstead's husband, Doctor Winstead, was there for a medical conference as a guest speaker. He missed all of it except the first day."

"Her husband missed the conference—that's all you got? Sorry but..." She sat up and the room spun around her. She shut her eyes, hoping to stop her stomach from revolting further. "Ahh."

"El?" Flash placed his hand on her back.

"I'm fine. It was just a bit much at first, but it's subsiding now." With a couple of deep breaths, she opened her eyes again to look at Rocco. "Can you get me a laptop or something? I'm tired of waiting for someone to get back to me. It's time for me to find out what happened to him. The FBI hired me for my skills and it's time I put that talent to use to help me, instead of someone else."

"That could cost you your job," Flash warned her.

"Or get you jailed."

"I spoke with her..." She dragged her hand through her hair. "Not even ten minutes before I got the call from Lewis, and she didn't say anything. She had to have known. Even once she approved Williams and the team to come here, nothing was said. I know at times you have to get a witness out of there in order to protect them, but the only reason I can think why he wouldn't find a way to let me know he was alive was if he were dying. If he's dying, I need to see him. This whole time when I thought he was dead, my one regret was that I never got to say goodbye."

"Give me a little more time and I'll have the information for you. I can do it without the consequence you'd face," Rocco urged.

"Sir." Tanner stood in the doorway, an e-tablet in his hand. "It's important. It's um...Don."

"Give me a minute," Rocco told them before quickly strolling toward the door.

"Flash, please, I need a laptop. Mine's back at my dad's house."

Before Flash could reply, Rocco turned back to them. "I'll get it for you but there's no need. Tanner, check El over and make sure she's able to fly. I'll call and have the plane standing by."

"What's going on? Fly...plane? I'm not going anywhere."

"You are if you want to see your dad." He handed the e-tablet back to Tanner. "Show her this. I need to get things organized. Elise, I'll have a laptop brought to you after Tanner examines you." With that, he was gone.

"Here." Tanner brought the tablet to them and as Flash took it, he tipped his head. "I'll step outside and give you a few minutes. Let me know when you're ready."

Her thoughts were running in two different directions. One moment she was thinking Dad was alive, otherwise Rocco wouldn't be ordering a plane. Then, Tanner's distant attitude made her question what she was about to find on the tablet. Her heart pounded against her chest, echoing in her ears, while serving to make her head spin more. There had been too much happening. Her body couldn't handle it.

"El." Flash held the tablet out to her and there, on the screen, was an image of her father on a gurney, his eyes closed and blood soaking through the sheet. "Focus and read below it."

She could see the words but that was as far as her brain would allow her to go. Her eyes stayed focused on her father's form on the gurney, searching for any sign of life. The photo held no sign of his chest rising and falling as he took a breath. A still image from a security camera, but it was enough to confirm her father hadn't died on the side of the road as Lewis had claimed.

"El, listen to me." He pulled the tablet from her hands and dropped it onto the bed. "He's alive."

"How do you know?"

"They have him sedated." He reached down, hit the power button on the tablet to take her attention off it, and placed his finger under her chin, forcing her to look up at him. "He was shot and suffered third degree burns on his legs, but he's alive. Doctor Winstead is a burn specialist and I believe since they couldn't bring him to New York without taking the chance Lewis would find him, they took him to Winstead."

"I have to go to him."

"I know, and Rocco's arranging it. But I need to know you're okay. You still seem out of it. You need to be honest with me; how bad are you still feeling the effects from the drugs?"

"Honestly, I feel like I'm in a fog. It takes my brain longer to comprehend what's happening, my vision is blurry, but the worst part is I feel as though my heart's going to beat out of my chest." Honesty was better than lying because if something happened once they left the penthouse, it would only make things worse. "My vision scares me the most. I can't focus; it's not quite double, but almost so and it's hazy. It's hard to describe, but I can't shoot like this—well, not accurately at least."

"Lucky for you, I'm here." He pressed his lips to her forehead. "Jac and Rocco's guards are here, too. You're as safe as they get. Now I'll get Tanner and I want you to let him give you something for the headache at least."

"Nothing too strong."

He slipped his arm out from around her and started to move off the bed. "Your vision is what made you think about shooting earlier, isn't it? When you were thinking about having to shoot Chang? You weren't actually planning to kill him."

"Yes...I mean no." She leaned back against the plush pillows. "I was thinking if Chang came after me, I wouldn't be able to shoot him without risking bystanders. Why?"

"Good. I was worried about the changes within you. I wasn't sure if this changed my sweet law-abiding girl or not."

"It's changed me." She fiddled with the hem of the blanket. "I'm not sure

I'm in the career I want. Maybe having a coworker betray you and those in charge letting you believe your father is dead is enough to make me walk away from everything."

"Well, you know there's a job opportunity on the table and it comes with an extra benefit." He slipped off the bed and shot her a cocky grin. "Me."

"What the hell?" She shot up, ignoring the nausea as she moved to the end of the bed. "What happened to you?"

"I guess you don't like my cockiness. Either way, you know the job still stands even if you don't want anything to do with me."

She grabbed a hold of his T-shirt and pulled him back to the bed. "You're bleeding."

"I'm fine." He touched his side.

"Bullshit." Tugging his shirt up, she didn't expect to see what she found. A couple inches above his hip was a slash wound; he had it covered over but the bandage was so wet with blood, it wasn't sticking. Her gaze traveled over the rest of his chest, taking in the extent of his other injuries. Mostly bruises but there was another wound, held close with butterfly bandages. The worst bruise was the one on his chest, just below the collarbone, where his shoulder met his chest—a deep purple and swollen. "This can't all be from last night. Some of this is from when you were in police custody."

"El, it's nothing."

"The hell it is." She rose on her knees and reached up to touch his face. Her fingers were met with the rough stubble running along his jaw. "I want whoever did this. This is abuse of their power. I'm going to find out who manufactured the evidence because Lewis couldn't have done all that himself. I'm going to see that they pay for it."

"None of it matters."

"It matters to me; *you* matter to me." In that moment, things started to slip into place and she looked up at him, letting their gazes lock. "Kiss me."

"El."

"I never thought I'd see you again, and yet here you are. So, shut up and kiss me." The last few days had been hell and she wasn't sure what she'd find in Pennsylvania. Right then, all she wanted was to feel alive.

He leaned into her until his lips were mere inches apart. "You sure?"

"There's only one other thing I've ever been this sure of." Not wanting to get into that, she closed the distance between them. Careful with his split lip, she kissed him tenderly. The moment their lips met, it was like all the time they'd been apart was gone.

He wrapped his arms around her, pressing her tight against the front of him. Surprised by the way his body was already reacting to her, she let out a gasp, opening her lips to him. He used that opportunity to slip his tongue between her lips and deepen their kiss. She ran her hands up his back as she pressed herself against him, wanting more. Their tongues danced together, each exploring the other's mouth, until she was breathless. With one final kiss, he ended the magic but didn't step away.

"Now, sweetie, what was the other thing you were so sure of?"

"Wouldn't you like to know." She leaned back and noted the blood on her shirt. "Wow, I just realized this isn't mine."

"El."

"The shirt. Whose is it? And it brings forth another issue; unless someone remembered to grab my bag from the house, I don't have anything to wear. The dress I wore to the funeral home was ruined."

"It's mine, so don't worry about it." His fingers teased along the hem, not moving the material up, but sending goosebumps through her all the same. "You look so fucking sexy in it. I hate to tell you there's stuff for you in the bathroom. It's not the stuff from the house, but it will work. Now sit back down and I'll get Tanner."

"I'll only let him check me over if you let him stitch up your wound." She placed her hand on his chest. "And afterwards I want to know what happened. How you ended up stabbed and what happened after Rocco took me out of the tunnel."

"You might be able to get your way with others, but you know it's never worked that way with me. I'll hold you down while Tanner examines you if I need to. Is that what you want?"

"Just so you know I've never been intimidated by you. But to make things easier, how about this? You let him deal with the wound, and I'll tell you about the other thing I was sure of. Deal?" She leaned back on the bed and without thinking, she slid her legs out from under her, landing on the side where she had been shot. Pain radiated through her. "Oh, shit!"

"Fuck, El." He lifted her up, getting her off the injury.

"I forgot…"

"It's painful but you were lucky it was a grazing wound, otherwise you could have bled out before we got there." He helped her sit down on the edge of the bed. "Let's get us both patched up and then go find Chief Dalton."

She waited until he strolled around the bed, heading for the door, before she called out to him. "One thing first. The other thing I've been completely sure about was…my love for you. You stole my heart when you came up to me in the lunchroom in ninth grade. After my father busted up a party the night before, everyone was pissed off at me and I was left sitting alone. I was sulking that his actions had my friends upset with me and you dropped down onto the chair next to me like you owned that table."

"My name was on it." He shot her a big goofy grin before continuing to the door.

Memories of sitting there at what had turned into their table flooded back to her. His name had been on it and by the end of that year, hers was carved into it, too. From that day forward, they were nearly inseparable. *Until he hopped onto his motorcycle and rode out of my life.*

Chapter Ten

Upon touching down at the municipal airport in the Pocono Mountains, they still didn't have a game plan. Elise spent most of the plane ride searching for her father, looking for any link they could follow. Rocco was on his phone doing much of the same thing. Still, they didn't have a solid lead.

"This is why we should have stayed in New York." Jac stood in the aisle watching her as she continued to work on the laptop. "Williams would have called once he had the information."

"You didn't have to come." This wasn't the first complaint she'd heard from him and it wouldn't be the last. He had been against this trip since she told him she was going but she wasn't letting him stop her.

"Are the drugs still effecting your ability to think? This could all be a setup. You don't know where this photo came from. As far as I know, Chang hasn't been arrested and you're taking risks when you don't have a solid lead. You're not risking just yourself, but all of us."

"Why don't you just say it? You're concerned that this will cost you your job." She sat the laptop on the seat beside her and rose. "I didn't ask you to come. Hell, Jac I suggested you stay in New York. This is my family and my fight. I couldn't sit and do nothing."

"My orders are to protect you. That's what I'm doing." His gaze lifted from hers to look past her but she didn't turn around. The plane door was still closed so anyone moving about had come with them.

"The image was from the clinic at which they treated Chief Dalton." Flash came up behind her and placed a hand on her shoulder. "It just so happens it was Doctor Flynn's clinic. Rocco and Flynn go way back."

"If he was transported here for Doctor Winstead, why would he be treated at this clinic, under another doctor?" Jac questioned, clearly not believing the information.

"Doctor Winstead was here for a conference. He didn't have the medical supplies he needed, but Doctor Flynn did. Lucky for us, Doctor Flynn set up practice here a couple of years ago and arrangements were made." Flash squeezed her shoulder. "We're going to be leaving."

"Not until I know what's going on. We need to put a plan together," Jac started in on Flash before she could even ask if Rocco had found a location.

"You're not in charge here, Agent." He pushed on her shoulder, moving her back in front of her seat, so that the men were facing each other.

"Stop it," she snapped. This sudden pissing contest between the two of them was enough to make her wish Jac had stayed in New York. "Flash is right; we both agreed to Rocco leading this mission. He's the one who found the information. We're using his contacts and his men. It's not his first mission, and this is what he does for a living. As for a plan, there isn't one. We're not storming the place to make arrests. I'm not here as an FBI agent; I'm here as a daughter."

"We're still agents." Jac grabbed his black suit jacket off the chair and shrugged it on. "At least for the moment. Come morning light, I don't know if that will be the case."

"I get it, and I'm fine with them taking my badge as long as I find my father. He'd do the same for me." She closed the laptop lid and slid it back into the bag Rocco had delivered it to her in. "I'm offering once again: you can stay here. No hard feelings. But if you get off this plane, then you accept that you're waist deep in this just like the rest of us and Rocco is in charge."

"I'm not leaving you." Jac shook his head. "I owe you this."

"You owe me nothing." She slipped the bag over her shoulder and stepped back into the aisle. "If we end up in a shit storm because of this, I'll do what I can to keep you out of it."

"You'd sacrifice yourself when it's my decision to back you?"

"Yeah. Loyalty is something I heard repeatedly from those in charge but when it came down to it, where was it? No one had my back. They let me believe my father was dead. I grieved, made funeral arrangements, attended the viewing, and would have put him into the ground if it wasn't for a few details we caught. In the end, this taught me something…" She glanced up at Flash before turning back to Jac. "There are things more important in life than work. Love, family, and friendships."

"Look at the bright side, Jac." Rocco's voice caused them to turn around to see him standing near the small drink area. "There's always a job waiting at Phantom Security. I can't promise we'll still have the government contract, but there's plenty of other work."

"I—" Her cell phone rang, cutting her off. Anticipation had her dropping the bag onto the seat and pulling the phone from the front zipper. *Unknown caller.* Instantly, her hope dissipated. Assistant Director Winstead, her team, and Williams' numbers were programed in and their names would have appeared on the screen, making it doubtful that this would be about her father or taking down Lewis's men.

"Go ahead," Flash encouraged.

With a deep breath, she brought the phone to her ear. "Special Agent Dalton."

"Elise—"

"Dad?" Her knees gave out and she sank to the floor in the middle of the aisle. "Dad, is that really you?" Flash squatted down behind her, his arms coming around her, comforting her.

"It's me. Where are you? They won't tell me anything. Are you safe? Lewis is dead but you need to stay away from Chang."

"Oh, Daddy!" Sitting in the middle of the walkway, tears streaming down her face, she felt like a little girl and couldn't wait for him to wrap his arms around her again. Knowing he was alive took a huge weight off her shoulders. Now she just had to get to him. "Where..." Her hand shook, causing her to drop the phone before she could finish her question.

"Here, El, let me." Flash grabbed the phone from the floor but before he could bring it to his ear, Rocco took it.

"No, you see to her. I'll find out where Chief Dalton is." Rocco took the phone from him and then stood back up. "Tanner, get a trace on this. Now!"

"Yes, sir."

"Chief Dalton, this is Rocco Arquette. I'm with your daughter, and I assure you she's safe. We've been looking for you. Do you know where you are?" As her father started to holler, Rocco took a couple of steps away from them. "I understand, sir, but the people you trust are compromised. If you give me your location, I can bring her to you."

"El." Flash pulled her to his chest, holding her. "He's alive—that's what matters. We'll get you to him."

"I can't believe it. I was preparing myself for the worst but he's alive." Relieved, she melted into his embrace but focused on Jac who was still standing in front of her. "Let Rocco fly you back to New York. No one will be the wiser that you were here. Tell them I slipped out while you were sleeping. Hell, tell them I drugged you. I don't care. This is my choice. You don't need to suffer the consequences."

"Screw that, Elise. We're partners; we're in this together." He sat the coffee mug on the small table by one of the seats and came toward them to squat down in front of her. "I'm with you. I believe they should have told you. We could have done things differently with the information. If we'd have known, we could have focused on the investigation into Lewis instead of Chief Dalton."

"Thank you, Jac." Without moving out of Flash's embrace, she reached out and placed her hand over Jac's. "That means a lot to me."

"Don't go soft on me," he teased. "Shit's about to hit the fan and I need you on your game."

"What are you implying?" Flash questioned but she didn't need Jac to answer; she already knew.

"Assistant Director Winstead isn't in the office; most likely she's with Dad. She's not our direct commander but she can still make our lives Hell." She eyed Jac again. "Last chance."

"Not happening. So, let's figure out how we're going to deal with her." He rose and held out his hand to her. "Then you're going to need to figure out how you're going to handle Chief Dalton."

"Dad?" She took Jac's hand and let him pull her up off the floor.

"He means because of me." Flash stood but stayed far enough away from her that they were no longer touching. "I don't like it, but I trust these guys to keep you safe."

"What are you saying?" She turned in the narrow aisle to look at him.

"He's offering to stay here." Rocco joined them again now that he was off the phone.

"Maybe it's not such a bad—" Jac started to add his input when she stopped him.

"Guys, can you give me a few minutes with Flash?" She looked at Rocco, hoping he'd take his guys and go to the two SUVs he had standing by.

"Outside, guys," he said with a nod, understanding what she was asking. "When you're ready, we'll move out. Chief Dalton didn't know where he was, but we've tracked the location. It's fifteen minutes away."

"You too, Jac," she told him as the rest started to disembark from the plane, but he stood there waiting. "Actually, Rocco, were you able to determine how he got the cell phone?"

"It's Doctor Winstead's. They wouldn't give Chief Dalton a phone, so when Doctor Winstead was doing his exam, your dad plucked it out of his pocket." He shook his head. "He's been advised to delete the call from the log and drop it down from the bed so it appears the doctor had dropped it. If they discover the phone, it won't appear he's made a call. Still, Elise, make this as quick as you can. If they move him before we get to him, they're going to cover their tracks better and we're going to have a harder time to find him."

"Five minutes." she told him and waited for Rocco and Jac to leave before she turned to Flash. "I need to know what's happening between us."

"What do you want to be happening?" Flash turned the question around on her before she could even get her thoughts in order.

"Flash…" She dropped down on the seat. The laptop bag sitting behind her meant she couldn't lean back but at least she wasn't about to drop to the floor again. It had been twenty-four hours but she still wasn't herself. Maybe it wasn't the drugs; maybe it was her adrenaline running out. "You know what? I'm tired of hiding my feelings so I'll just lay it all out there."

Taking a couple of deep breaths, she calmed the roar of her heart beating in her ears. "When you left, you broke my heart. Everyone kept telling me I was too young to know what true love was. I'd get over you and find the one I was supposed to be with. Except that never happened. You were my one. I never stopped loving you. When you were in jail, I dug into the case not because I wanted justice for my father, which I did, but also because I couldn't believe you did it. Then, when you showed up, it was like nothing had changed."

"Really? Because I seem to remember you had a gun pointed at me." She jerked her head up to look at him, only to find him leaning against a chair, grinning at her. "You going to deny it?"

"Asshole." Even as she bitched, she couldn't stop the smile from spreading over her face. "You were attacking an FBI Special Agent. You should be glad he didn't shoot you."

"Don't worry, he tried, but I'm quicker. It also helped I knew going in he'd be armed. He didn't know who would be at the door, and I don't think you considered the danger you were in then; otherwise, he'd have been on guard."

"I had bigger priorities. You know, like trying to get your sorry ass out of jail." She stood and strolled back toward the small drink area across from the lavatory, to grab a bottle of water from the mini-fridge. "What were you thinking?"

He was behind her as she stood, his hands caressing over her hips. "You, El."

"What?" She couldn't think with his breath on her neck and his hands teasing along her body.

"Sweetie, you're always on my mind. Over the years, I've hoped you'd settle down with a man that could be what your dad wanted for you. Someone like Jac." He spit the last part out, as if he couldn't stand the very thought of them together. "When Lewis said he was coming after you, that he had someone watching you, I could only think of the man who was with you at the station. I wanted him dead for hurting you when he should be protecting you. Once I got him out of the way, I was going to whisk you away to somewhere safe so I could deal with Lewis."

"I don't need protecting."

"You don't get it." He spun her around so they were facing each other and pressed her back against the lavatory door. "I fucking love you, El. I left the last time because it was best for you. You deserved things I couldn't give you, no matter how much I wanted to."

"All I've ever wanted was you." Trailing her fingers along the curve of his jaw, she was met by rough stubble. "Last time I was this close to you, you were clean shaved."

"That's when I was trying to impress your father." He tipped his head to kiss the palm of her hand. "You know what's going to happen if I go with you."

"Yes, and I also know that I wouldn't be here without you. You saved my life. Need another reason? Well, here you go. If you're going to be part of my life, we're going to have to face him sooner or later. I want you in my life and nothing Dad will say is going to change that. I love you, Flash. So, unless you're planning on hopping back on your motorcycle and pealing out of my life again, I want you there with me."

"Fuck that." He leaned down so his lips were hovering above hers. "I don't have the willpower now to keep myself from you again. You're stuck with me, sweetie, unless you're going to shove me away."

"Not a chance." She closed the distance between them and pressed her lips to his.

Their lips had barely touched when he pulled back with a groan. Arching forward, he pressed his body against her. "You feel that, baby? You feel my hard cock pressed against you. That's what you do to me. It's taking the last bit of willpower within me not to keep everyone waiting and fuck you right here. To give you something to remind you of me when your old man lays in on you, so you'll remember we're worth fighting for."

"Give me a little bit longer and I'll take care of that for you." She was tempted to slip her hand between them, to feel his hardness, but he kept her pinned against the door, leaving no room between them for such movements. It was for the best but it deprived her of something she wanted desperately.

"I'll hold you to that." He stepped back and she could see his body's reaction. "Keep looking at me like that, El, and we won't make it off this plane. Now move; we've got to go."

Keeping her hands to herself, she slipped past him and grabbed the bag off the chair before turning back to look at him. "One more thing. I thought you should be the first to know. I'm leaving the bureau. They can call it selfish or blame it on regulations—I don't care. What happened cut too deep for me to continue with them. I've lost faith in them. Going into an assignment without all available information could get someone killed. They can say I was there on leave to deal with a family emergency, but the team wasn't. When this is over, if Rocco's job offer is still on the table, I'm going to accept it."

"What do you say to working on my team?" He slipped his hand into hers, interlacing their fingers. "I can't stand the thought of being separated from you for weeks while we're gone."

"I could be tempted. It depends on the benefit package."

"My sweet El, I promise you it will be worth it. But there's one more thing you need to realize before we see your father. I can't return to Pinewood. Not if we want a fresh start. They'll always consider me a murderer; they convicted me already. I know that's home to you and means a lot to you."

"Not as much as you mean to me. Screw Pinewood. Plus, it looks like we'll be working in New York City and that kind of commute would suck. We'll find a place together...I mean, unless..."

"The way you nibble on the corner of your lip when you're uncertain is so completely fucking sexy. Shit, what am I saying? Everything you do turns me on."

"You're sex starved." She shook her head.

"For you, sweetie." He tucked the strand of hair that came out of her clip behind her ear. "We got off track. I want you with me always. I want you in my arms each night. We've got a lot of time to make up for."

With a smile on her face, they walked out of the plane, hand in hand. They had lost too much time but they were given a second chance, in more ways than one. With every door that closed around them, another one opened, leading them to the life she always believed they should have had—a life together.

Chapter Eleven

Sitting in the SUV a quarter mile from Chief Dalton had Flash apprehensive. He had El back in his life and he wasn't about to give her up again without a fight, but whatever happened in the next few hours could change things. Chief Dalton didn't want Flash anywhere near his daughter and even after El had said nothing would divide them, he couldn't help but be concerned. The anxiousness pouring off her made him wonder if she was worried about it, too.

Rocco had Tanner and Brady doing a scan of the property before they moved in. They needed the intelligence in order to ensure things would go smoothly. For El, he hoped Dalton wasn't in dire condition. He called her and sounded lucid but that didn't mean he was out of the woods yet. They didn't know what state he was in or what kind of treatment he was getting. Chief Dalton might hate his guts but he wasn't about to be scared off by a couple of FBI agents. He'd make sure El's father was receiving the care he needed and would make a full recovery. Eventually, she'd have to bury him but after everything she'd already gone through, it wasn't going to be now.

He watched as she slipped her weapon from the laptop bag and after checking to make sure it was loaded, she slipped it back into the harness and into the waistband of her pants. She might not have realized but she was apprehensive about what they would encounter there. All her life, she'd lived by the book; before now, the only time she'd wavered from it was their brief time together. Now she was taking the biggest detour of her life and he couldn't help but think that some of this was his fault. He hadn't even been in town when Chief Dalton was attacked, but he'd played into it.

She might be willing to do this even though it was an unauthorized mission but he'd do his best to make sure she didn't set her career on fire. One day, working for Phantom Security might not be enough for her and she might want to return to the FBI. If that day came, he wasn't sure how things would work for them, but the most important thing to him was El. He wanted her happy, even if that meant she wasn't with him.

Like her, he had a gun strapped to his belt. Legally, he was allowed to carry it now, so he didn't have to hide it like the last time he'd come up against law enforcement. Even if he had to carry illegally, he wasn't going to take her into a situation where he couldn't protect her. Not after Mick kidnapped her to deliver her to Lewis. Could they trust Assistant Director Winstead? Doctor Winstead? After they'd betrayed El, he didn't believe they could, but he knew Winstead would blame it on regulations. To him, that wasn't enough.

"Okay." Rocco turned slightly in his seat to look at Jac who occupied the passenger seat, and then back to El and him in the backseat. "There are three people in the house. Chief Dalton is in the back bedroom. The other two are in the living area. Tanner believes the woman is Assistant Director Winstead. She's at the table with her laptop. We're going to assume the other is Doctor Winstead, but he could be another agent. At least one of them is armed, but remember who they are. Don't shoot unless you have no other options."

"I still think you should let me go alone." She tried again even though it was pointless; they'd already had the argument.

"No." Rocco looked at him for a moment and he wasn't sure if he was hoping he'd back him on what he was about to say or if Rocco was worried Flash was about to flip. "Unless we walk up to the house, they're going to know we're coming. The road is in plain sight of the house and there are no other residences back there."

"Walking could put us in additional danger. If we found this location, Chang or someone under Lewis might have as well. They could be in the woods, waiting," Jac reasoned.

"Tanner and Brady did a scan but they didn't have enough time to eliminate all possibilities." Flash took her hand into his, trying to reassure her. "We'll drive. We have no reason to sneak up on them and we might need the SUVs."

"Okay, then here's how this is going to go. We drive up there and I want the two of you to stay in the vehicle until we know it's safe." Rocco's gaze stayed on him.

"Why?" She shifted in her seat, clearly uneasy with the tension rising in the confined space.

"The same reason you just strapped on your weapon." Flash squeezed her hand. "They're not going to know who's outside and they're on guard. Rocco and Jac she knows. You're his daughter but after the last angry message you left her, she's not going to be sure what your intentions are. Then there's me. She might know I didn't kill Chief Dalton, but she's not a fan of mine."

"That might have something to do with you throwing her agent through a glass window." Rocco raised an eyebrow at him.

"I was trying to protect Lexi," he growled. "I didn't know he was an undercover agent. All I knew was he came bashing into the hotel lobby and I had to protect her."

"Fine. Let's just do this." She waited until Rocco put the SUV into drive and began to pull back on the road before she turned back to him. "Do you make it a habit of attacking FBI agents? So far, the count is two. Any more I need to know about?"

"Does the attack I'm planning for you later count?"

"No." She leaned back against the seat and tipped her head to rest along the side of his arm. "I won't be with the bureau then."

"What?" Jac turned to look back at her. "You're turning in your badge?"

"I've known from the beginning I wouldn't walk away from this with my badge."

"You've worked hard to get where you are, and you're just going to let them strip it away from you without a fight?"

"It is what it is." She shrugged. "I realized there's more to life. Family. Good friends. When's the last time you saw your little girl? When's the last time you've had her for the whole weekend you're supposed to get? Why...because of this job. There's more to life than this and until now I've been happy with my life. I've loved my job but all of this changed something within me. They turned their back on me and now it's time for a change."

"You're going to let her throw away her career?" Jac glanced at him.

"I'll support her no matter what she wants. If she wants to leave the FBI, there's somewhere else she can put her skills to use. I know my El; she's talented and the FBI was lucky to have her. She's not just handy with computers, though her ability to find the dirt on anyone is insane, and she can hack into anyone's system. She can also protect herself. Her legal knowledge surpasses that of some of the lawyers I know, and that's saying something considering the beasts Rocco's hired."

"I can't believe this." Jac turned back to the road as the house came into view.

"I love you, El, and no matter what you choose, you have my support." He pressed his lips to the top of her head. "Are you ready for this?"

"Let's do this." She leaned forward and ran her hands over her black slacks clad thigh.

"Stay close to me until we know." He adjusted in his seat. "Hell, stay close to me always."

"There's nowhere I'd rather be," she whispered, dragging her hand up his leg.

The simple touch already had his shaft hardening. *Fuck, she's going to be the*

Rage erupted through Elise at the sight of Assistant Director Winstead standing in the doorway looking as though she should be on her way to the office, instead of protecting her father. Her short brown hair, curled so it framed her face, made her look younger. Her black skirt suit with low black heels reminded her that the assistant director hadn't been in the field in years. What was she thinking protecting Chief Dalton alone, with no backup? Unable to keep her promise to Rocco and stay in the vehicle, she grabbed the door handle and hopped out before Flash could stop her.

"Damn it, El." He didn't bother to get out his door and go around; rather, he followed her out the same side.

"I should have known you were behind this." Assistant Director Winstead's gaze landed on her. "Your skills don't make up for your stupidity. What were you thinking, coming here?"

"I was thinking about my father. You know, the one I was supposed to be burying but who is alive and inside that house." She stalked forward, ignoring the side eye she was getting from Jac. "Maybe I should ask you what you were thinking? What gave you the right to let me believe I was burying my father? Do you have any idea what I've suffered through the last few days?"

"Regulati—"

"Fuck your regulations!" She was fuming and no amount of deep breaths were going to calm her. "I was in danger and no one bothered to warn me. But that's not even the worst part. You let Williams lead the team into the same situation without telling them what was happening. You put every single one of us in jeopardy. There was no reason for it. With the information you held back from us, we could have done the same thing we did, but with precautions to keep us safe and without us wasting time looking into what you already knew."

"Decisions were made and I stand by them."

"I figured you'd say that." She shook her head. "Sitting up in that office has made you forget what it's like in the field. You're not the one taking the risks, we are, and every detail you don't tell us puts us in that much more danger."

"This time the cost was the lives of two agents." Jac took a step closer to her. "And almost cost us a third."

"Two?" Assistant Director Winstead spoke before Elise could question Jac's comment.

"Mick Lee, and a short time ago I was informed that Mel Ward succumbed to the gunshot wound she received in the raid. That's just from our team, I don't know if there were any other casualties."

The loss of Mel threw Elise off her game for a moment, while at the same time enticing the rage within her. She glanced down at her finger, where she still wore the borrowed engagement ring from Mel. Being another FBI agent, Mel's fiancé understood the dangers of their work all too well, but it would do nothing to subside the grief.

"What raid?"

"You've got to be kidding me!" Assistant Director Winstead's question enraged her enough to take another step forward. "I was fucking drugged and I know what he's talking about. You would too if you listened to your voicemail."

"When we rescued Elise, there was information of a scheduled prostitute drop happening soon. Williams, Mel, and the other team you had in Pinewood followed up on it. They'd hoped Chang would be there and they could take him down, but he wasn't. Others were there, but besides Mel's death and the prostitutes saved, I have no other information. Williams didn't go into who was arrested or if anyone was injured or killed. If you want further details, you'll have to contact them yourself. My duty was to protect Elise." Jac nodded toward the house. "Maybe we should take this inside. Chang is still free and I suspect he'll want to tie up loose ends so he doesn't end up in prison."

"Then you need to get back to New York and take him down before he has the chance." Assistant Director Winstead crossed her arms over her chest, blocking the doorway.

"Why don't you?" Elise snapped.

"Elise is angry right now, but there's no reason to have this showdown. We know Chief Dalton is inside and that's why we're here. It would be best for everyone involved if you just let us in." Rocco's voice held a warning.

"He's right, dear." An older man came up behind her and placed his hand on her shoulder. "Chief Dalton called them."

"How? I took his…" She spun back to her husband as if things had finally clicked. "Tell me you didn't."

"I told you she had a right to know. His condition is improving but we almost lost him once. If that were your father, you'd want to be with him during his last moments." He guided his wife out of the doorway and nodded for them to come inside. "He's in the back bedroom. I have him on strong pain relievers so he might not be awake now, but he comes in and out of it."

After they stepped inside and Jac closed the door behind them, she turned to the doctor. "How bad is it?"

"When the bomb went off it threw him away from the cruiser. Unfortunately, he slammed into something, breaking two of his ribs. It's possible he lost consciousness after the blast because he doesn't remember what he hit. He could also be blocking that memory. The burns on his legs are what I'm worried about. Second and third degree burns span up both limbs, causing him significant pain."

"Why would he block the memory of what happened? How did you find him before Pinewood Fire Department? They were first on the scene." She looked from Doctor Winstead to his wife before asking the last question. "Who was the man I almost buried as my father?"

"I brought Chief Dalton into this, so if you're looking for someone to blame, blame me," Assistant Director Winstead told her. "I needed someone close to Lewis to gather the evidence. The ones we sent in were only able to get so close and it was taking too long."

"You're avoiding the questions she asked you." Flash's hand touched the small of her back and she had a brief moment to wonder if he was keeping his touch hidden to keep things calm or if it was unintentional.

"He was meeting with his contacts Agent Hunt and Agent Bryne. Dalton asked for the meeting, to follow up on the image that was sent to us. Lewis had to know Dalton was working with us. The bomb was intentional, with the goal of killing Dalton before any further information could be given to us. The bomb went off at the precise time Chief Dalton should have been on his way to work." She shifted her weight and wouldn't meet Elise's gaze. "Agent Bryne was killed."

"Dad lives by a routine. He always leaves the house the same time each day to arrive at the station. Lewis would have known Dad would be in his patrol car then. Even with this break in his routine to meet with Agents Bryne and Hunt, that routine almost killed him."

"If he knows Lewis is behind all this, why would be block out the memory of the bombing?" Flash pressed.

"My medical theory is watching Agent Bryne burn was more than he can face now. Subconsciously, he knows it should have been him," Doctor Winstead explained.

"In Agent Hunt's quick thinking, he loaded Chief Dalton into his car and hightailed it out of there before anyone could be any the wiser. His quick action possibly saved your father's life. So instead of you blaming the FBI, you should be thankful Dalton is still alive." Assistant Director Winstead stalked over to the kitchen table and sat down.

"I'm grateful to Agent Hunt, and I'm sorry about Agent Bryne. It's you I'm pissed at. My father spoke highly of you and he was excited that I would be working on one of the teams you oversaw. Even if we didn't have much direct communication, he figured just having you oversee things would somehow keep me safer. That gave him the peace of mind he needed because he never wanted me working in the field. He wanted me to take an office position and use my computer skills, but it wasn't enough for me. I wanted the action. Now you can justify what you did however you'd like, but on some level, you have to realize what you did was wrong." She glanced back to Flash and Rocco. "I'm going to see him now. Are you coming?"

Flash nodded and she held out her hand to him. She wasn't sure if he was trying to hide what was happening between them or not but she wanted his touch. He took her hand and pulled her close. Any doubt that he didn't want anyone to know about them was gone.

"Thank you." Even with her being a good four inches shorter than him, they were close enough that she could feel his breath caress along her check.

"You two seem awful close. The criminal accused of murdering Chief Dalton and the Chief's daughter…oh, I'm sure the residents of Pinewood are going to love that." Assistant Director Winstead's deep heckling laugh proved enough for her to spin back around to face her.

"Is he the one Lewis arrested?" Doctor Winstead came close to the table.

"Yes, he's the man your wife let sit in jail for days being attacked by Lewis's crew. Did your source inform you what they were doing to him? Or were you avoiding their calls, too?"

"What have you done, dear?" He sat down at the head the table, his gaze on his wife.

"What I had to do." There was no remorse in Assistant Director Winstead's voice, yet she wouldn't look up at them.

"How many times would you have taken being beaten or stabbed before you broke down and told them whatever they wanted to know?" she pressed, not willing to give up. "Through it all he never said anything about the investigation or even his alibi. Flash Arquette is a better person than you will ever be. He protected those that didn't deserve his protection."

"I'd trust him at my back over you any day." Jac eyed the assistant director. "I've got into some fucked up situations with both of you, but with him, I never questioned him being there, doing what needed to be done. You, Winstead are weak; you're not worthy of command. You don't see the people under you; you only see how to get another case closed. You risk your people when there are other options and that's why you have the highest injury on the job status of any other director. You're a danger to those who are under you."

"Come on, El, let's see your father." Flash took a step forward, his hand still in hers, urging her forward. "None of this matters."

It mattered to her and the topic wasn't closed but right then seeing her father was more important. There would be time to speak with Assistant Director Winstead later.

"I'll check the room and then give you time with him." Rocco told her before looking past her toward the table. "Afterward, I'd like a moment of your time, Assistant Director Winstead. There are a few things we need to discuss."

"I'll stay on guard here." Jac turned away from the Winsteads to look out the window. "Focus on your dad; we'll make sure you're safe."

"You believe we're in danger here?" Doctor Winstead asked.

"If Chang has found the location, then yes." She started toward the hallway but glanced back at the doctor. "Until Chang is caught and some questions are answered, I don't know if I believe anywhere is safe. I was kidnapped from my father's house by a man I trusted, fellow agent Mick Lee. So, doctor, please forgive me if I've lost my confidence in your wife. For all I know, she's given the location to these people. I trust Jac, Rocco, Flash, and Rocco's men outside. There's not a single doubt in my mind that they will do the job."

The sorrow in his eyes made her feel sorry for him. He was finding out the worst parts of his wife and because of the mess she created, he could be in danger. It might have been wrong of Elise but she didn't care about the woman. She had let people rot in jail while she continued to build her case. If she hadn't been able to gather the information she needed, would Flash still be in jail? She suspected he would be and that made her want to cling tighter to him.

Chapter Twelve

The house had three additional bedrooms and even though Elise wanted to stay near her father until he woke up, she agreed to take the second bedroom on the first floor. Flash would share it with her and the rest of them would use the upstairs room or crash on the sofa. It would work out fine since Rocco had his guys on shifts for her protection.

"You should try and rest." Flash sat their bags on the cedar chest at the edge of the bed. "Sitting there worrying isn't going to change anything. The medication won't wear off any faster whether you're sitting by his bedside or sleeping in the next room. I can keep watch and wake you when he starts to come out of it."

"You're too good to me." She dragged her hands through her hair, forcing it away from her face as she gently rocked in the rocking chair.

"I know a whole town that would disagree with you."

"They don't know you. With your shaggy hair, tattooed skin, and penetrating gaze, you're my knight in a leather jacket." She rose out of the chair and crossed the room to stand in front of him. "You keep it hidden, but you've got a soft, caring side. You rushed to my side when you thought I was in danger. After you rescued me from Lewis, you stayed close, watching over me. You cared for me when I became violently ill from the drugs and when I woke, you were there waiting."

"We can't let that get out or my reputation would be ruined." His lips curled into a smile as he looped his arms around her waist.

"My hardened bad boy has a soft side and I love it." She slipped her hands under the back of his shirt and let her hands caress up his back. "Even now when you're exhausted you're offering to watch over my father so I can sleep. You're the only one who'd do that."

"You've been through Hell and there are still lingering side effects from the drugs." He shook his head as she started to say something. "Don't deny it. I've seen you sway on your feet, so you still have moments of dizziness when you're standing and your headache is still there. You might be hiding more from me, but that, at least, I know. Sleeping will help."

"Sleep would help you, too."

"I'm fine," he tried to convince her but his body was betraying him.

"Now who's denying the facts?" She shook her head. "At best, in the last few days you've gotten a couple of hours of sleep the whole time. I know they didn't let you sleep when they had you in custody. Lewis was convinced if he had more time to work you, he'd break you and you'd confess."

"Don't think about that, El. It's in the past."

"When I saw you standing there shackled and wearing that orange jumpsuit, I thought I'd never feel your arms around me again. The hatred in your eyes made me believe I'd lost you for good. How can I not think about it? Everything you went through…"

"Brought me you and that, I wouldn't change. The hatred you saw was never meant for you, but when I saw Jac's arms around you, comforting you, I nearly snapped. That should have been me. It was supposed to be us together but I'd fucked up." He paused and let out a deep sigh before shaking his head. "My life was incomplete without you to share it with. Now that I have you, I'm never letting you go. The question is, will you still love a former bad boy who's given up his demons to live a law-abiding life? Well, as close to law-abiding as I can get working for Rocco."

"I've always loved you and will continue to every day for the rest of our lives. But maybe you could help this by-the-book girl venture into the gray areas a little more." She let out a light laugh. "It would kill my dad if I got arrested, so let's not go quite that far."

"I think lately you've been doing fine on your own." His fingers hooked on the hem of her shirt and he tucked it upward until he found skin. "If neither of us are going to sleep…"

"I love it when you steal the words out of my mouth." She tugged his shirt up, forcing him to let go of her so she could pull it over his head. "I want you and I'm tired of waiting." Butterflies danced in her stomach as anticipation grew.

"Once I get you naked and bury my cock between your legs, I'm never letting you go. So you need to be sure about this." Even as he spoke, he pulled her shirt up over her head. "Once I'm balls deep in you, you're mine. I'll never get enough of you."

"Good because all other women are off limits," she teased, knowing he'd never cheat on her. He might have done things in his past that she didn't agree with but he was faithful. Unhooking her belt, she pulled her holstered gun off and sat it on the bedside table.

"You're the only one I want." He slid the zipper down on her slacks before pushing them over her hips to fall around her ankles. "You're the woman I want by my side every day and in my bed every night."

"There's nowhere I would rather be than by your side for the rest of my life. We've had a hell of a road to get us here, but we're together again and every day, we'll make the most of it." In only her bra and panties, she climbed onto the bed.

Without saying a word, he placed his gun next to hers and stripped out of the rest of his clothes to stand before her completely naked. Needing to see him, all of him, she rose up onto her elbows. He'd had a great body the last time they were together, but now it was simply amazing. She ached to run her hand along his chest, to feel every chiseled aspect of his toned body. She wanted to take in every new tattoo that permanently marked his skin, but more than anything she wanted to touch the one she knew was there. The one that meant the most to them. She'd seen it back at Rocco's, but that was before she knew where things stood between them, and she hadn't wanted to bring up painful memories. Now there was nothing holding her back. Before he got dressed again, she needed to touch it.

"Come here." Excitement surged through her as she held out her hand to him.

"Do you remember the first time?" He climbed onto the bed next to her, his gaze never leaving hers.

"Like it was yesterday." She pressed him back onto the bed so that he was lounging back on the pillows and she knelt beside him. With her hands, she caressed over his chest, while tracing the lines of his tattoos—not yet nearing the special one, but rather exploring the new dark ink. "We were outside of town at Chesterfield park; there was a little field on the other side of the trees. From there you could see the rows of houses and they looked so small from up there. That night, the lights from Pinewood were nowhere near the brilliance of the stars in the sky, and the summer heat had nothing on the fire that burned between us."

"Making love to you under the stars is one of the memories that got me through the years. It kept me sane during my stint in prison."

"Are you implying you jerked off to the memory of us having sex?" She grinned down at him. "Why does the thought of that turn me on?"

"Because you like knowing you're the one woman I wanted. Not that I had much choice behind bars, but that wasn't the only time I replayed that night in my head. You were so fucking beautiful in that yellow sundress." Grabbing her wrist, he moved her hand down his body until she could feel his manhood. "Look at what you do to me. You make me so fucking hard."

"Let me take care of you." She wrapped her hand around his length.

"El…" A soft moan escaped his lips as she slid up his cock. "You don't know how amazing that feels, but first I want you naked. I want to see you spread out before me and know that you're as wet and ready for this as I am." He reached behind her, unhooked her bra, and stripped it from her in one clean move.

"Why don't you feel and find out?" she teased.

"Soon." He leaned forward, his arms wrapped around her waist, then kissed her—a long, slow deliberate kiss that gave and demanded. He cupped her breasts and teased her nipples, gently swirling his thumb against the hard buds and then pinching them. Pain mingled with pleasure and she arched into his body. He abandoned her mouth and kissed her neck, nibbling down her jawline to her shoulder. Slowly, he teased kisses down her chest until he came to her breast and flicked his tongue over her hardened nipple. The pleasure forced a moan from deep within her as she pressed against him. It felt as if every nerve ending in her body was alight with desire; the simplest touches fanned the burning need within her. Looking up at her, he sucked the nipple into his mouth, allowing his teeth to run along either side, before he let the hardened bud slip from his lips.

"I've missed how your body responds to my touch." Bringing her down onto the bed, he continued to caress her body. He teased along her flat stomach until he found the top of her panties. "You told me to find out, so lift your hips up."

She rose off the bed and after he slid the silky material down, she kicked them off, tossing them somewhere off the bed. His gaze traveled over her body, making her want to squirm, but she stayed still. "It's not the same body as before but I hope you like what you see."

"Every fucking inch of you is beautiful." He slid his hand down the curve of her hip and he traced along the only tattoo she'd ever got. The one he'd encouraged her to have done, while at the same time getting himself one. They were tied together with meaning to them. His was over his heart because to him, that was the only place it could have been. She had his heart and in place, he had the jigsaw puzzle piece she'd designed. "This was true then and is still true now."

She lifted her head to glance down at him and her own jigsaw puzzle piece tattoo. Unlike every other time she looked at it, she didn't feel her chest tighten with the loss of him. The three-fourths of a house that filled her piece was no longer unfinished now that he'd returned to her. She could picture the two pieces together again. In his, the two paths met to form one before leading up to part of the house that would be finished in hers. Hers was the only one with words as if to remind her what he always said. *With you, I'm home.*

The swirling part around each of their pieces served to remind them that no matter what was going on around them, they could come through it together. Together they were stronger than any mountain trying to divide them. They hadn't heeded that advice before, but they would this time. The piece they'd had tattooed on their skin years ago would be the future they'd claim now.

"Flash…I need…" Balancing herself on her elbow, she reached toward him, pushing him back so she could see his puzzle piece. Seeing it before, she hadn't allowed herself to take it in but now she realized he had added to it. The dark gray and black puzzle piece that fit into her brighter one—another way he showed how his life had brightened when she came into it—was now joined by a blood red heart that read: Owned by: Elise Dalton. Always.

"Flash…"

"I added it after I left. My chest felt empty and every day was hazy. I wanted to jump back on my motorcycle and come back to you, but I thought I was doing the right thing."

She pressed her finger to his lips. "Forget the past and make love to me."

Not needing any further encouragement, he trailed his hand down her body and between her thighs. The caresses of his fingers had her spreading her legs, and her breath caught in her chest. He explored up her inner thigh, ever so slowly, until he slipped his finger between her folds, quickly finding her center and working deep within her. His thumb brushed along her clit, sending fire through her body.

"Fuck, sweetie. A few caresses and you're already ready for me. You make me feel like I have a map to your body."

The ability to speak was gone, leaving her unable to respond to him. A moan tore from her as he worked a second finger into her. In and out, quicker with every pump. As her climax approached, he slowed, until he stopped altogether.

"Flash...I need you." Her hands were on his sides, and until she felt the bandage brush against her thumb, she hadn't thought about his stab wound. Her eyelids sprang open and she pulled her hands away from him. "I'm sorry."

"I'm fine, El. Don't pull away from me."

"I don't want to hurt you." She wiggled against him. "You get me so worked up I can't think. You know how I love to dig my nails into you."

Easing his way back up the length of her body, he blazed a trail of kisses across her stomach, stroking his fingertips along the curves of her sides. With every touch, she arched her hips into him, demanding more. "I love when you do that. The claw marks you leave on me as you're climaxing are a reminder of the pleasure we've shared. It's a papercut, nothing more. I want you like never before. I want you moaning my name until we're both out of breath and exhausted. Don't hold back on me now, El."

Papercut my ass. But the words died on her tongue as his thumb brushed along her clit, teasing her enough to have her lift her hips off the bed. She pressed against his hand, keeping it there, as her body rocked back and forth, forcing the pace faster. "Please, Flash..."

"Please what? Faster? Slower? Maybe you want me to stop." He stopped moving and even though she was still wiggling against his hand, it wasn't the same. He knew just where to touch her to make her melt.

"Asshole!" She growled at him, hating him for denying her what her body needed so badly.

"Well then, if that's what you think." His thumb brushed along her clit one final time before he pulled his hand away from her.

Shocked by the loss of his touch, she opened her eyes, only to find him grinning down at her. The cocky grin stretched across his face made her wish she had the willpower to get up and get dressed, leaving him without sex. He might be able to jerk off but it wouldn't be the same. "You better be glad I'm not into self-denial or I'd leave you high and dry right about now."

"Too bad that's what I'm doing to you." He pulled back but she grabbed his arm before he could get too far. "What?"

"Do you really think after you teased me I'd let you get away that easy?" She reached between them and wrapped her fingers around his cock, applying just enough pressure to force a moan from him, but not enough to hurt. "You're going to please me and I'll decide if I'm going to leave you with blue balls or not."

"You're so fucking sexy when you take control. So demanding and all I want to do is roll you onto your back and fuck you until you can't walk straight."

"What are you waiting for?" She leaned back against the pillows, willing him to make his move. "Come on, big boy."

As he slipped into place on top of her, she brought her legs up on either side of him and lazily dragged one hand along the side of his chest. Her fingers teased along his ribs but it was the contour of his muscles that she was enjoying. The tight muscles contracted under her touch, showing off the beauty of his chest. He worked hard to bulk up and she admired it. Her time in the gym was out of necessity, not out of enjoyment.

His chest vibrated as he chuckled and she looked up at him. "What?"

"I love that look on your face, but I can't help but wonder if you're in the mood for this. See, I'm about to shove my dick into your tight pussy and you're staring at my chest as though you haven't seen it before. It could give a man a complex."

"Really now?" She shook her head. "Trust me, I want this. I was only thinking that the last time you were in this position you didn't have his amazing body. It makes me want to drag my tongue along the contours of your chest."

"I wouldn't want to deprive you, so I think we can find time for that." He teased the tip of his dick along her slit before he arched forward, shoving it into her pussy in one quick movement, clearly telling her conversation time was over; all he wanted out of her was moans and her screaming his name.

A moan tore from her chest as her core muscles stretched to accommodate his width. "Flash!" Breathlessly, she ran her hands up his chest and let her body adjust.

Staring down at her, he slowly pumped his hips, sliding his dick in and out of her. Using one arm to keep himself hovered above her, he brought his other hand to her breast. He groaned as his fingers found her hard nipples. Rolling the hardened bud between his fingers, pinching it with enough pressure to have her arching forward, he increased his pace. Each pump of his hips had him going harder and faster, stealing her breath as her climax neared. Heat coiled between her thighs and her sex clenched around him.

"Please...faster!" She lifted her body up to meet his.

"You feel so fucking good wrapped around my dick. I've missed this." He pulled nearly his full length out, before slamming back into her. When he did, he sped his pace up. Their bodies rocked back and forth, each thrust gaining momentum, drawing her closer to her orgasm.

As if knowing she was close but needed more to push her over the edge, he reached between them, his thumb instantly finding her clit. But that wasn't enough for him; he dipped his head, his lips wrapping around her nipple to suck it in between his teeth. He swirled his tongue around the bud before his teeth closed down around it.

"Oh…Flash," she hissed in a mixture of pain and pleasure. Her climax was almost upon her as she arched forward, sending his dick deeper in her.

"Look at me, El. I want your eyes on me. I want you to know it's my dick in you, bringing you to your orgasm." His voice sounded strained as if he was close to his own orgasm but wouldn't give in until she had her release first.

"Flash," she whispered, her climax within reach. "Faster, please…" Her nails raked down his chest.

With one last flick over her clit, he leaned back, placing both hands on her hips, and pounded into her faster. She wrapped her legs around him, locking her ankles together at the small of his back, which kept him from pulling back too far. Tension had her muscles constricting around him as her orgasm neared, urging him to engage an even faster rhythm, and his eyes glazed over with his own ecstasy creeping up on him.

Keeping her gaze locked on his, she pressed her body to his. Her fingers tangled in his longer strands, bringing his head down so she could claim his lips. Slipping her tongue in between his lips, she moaned his name as her release found her. With her free hand, she raked the skin along his chest, digging her nails into his flesh.

Her core muscles tightened around him and she could feel the tension release from him as he slammed into her one final time before leaning forward against her and letting go, filling her. He buried his face in the arch of her shoulder. "Fuck, El."

"Mmm…now I know I can't ever let you go." With her fingers still in his hair, she let the palm of her hand brush along the side of his face. Her muscles continued to tighten around him, milking his cock for every drop. "I love you, Flash."

"My sweet, sexy El. I love you more than words could describe. I will spend every day of my life proving to you just how much I love you."

The idea of spending the rest of her life with him sent her heart fluttering. It was what she always wanted but never thought she'd have. *I'm not letting you go now, Flash Arquette. You're stuck with me. Forever.*

Chapter Thirteen

Hours of sitting by her father's bedside had left Elise exhausted. Every time she closed her eyes, she'd wake up with her heart pounding in her chest, afraid something had happened and she missed him being awake. Unwilling to take a nap, she needed more coffee. With Flash asleep in the recliner that sat in the corner of the room, she tiptoed out of the room. The sun was starting to peek over the horizon, leaving the house quiet as everyone slept.

With the early hour, she hoped she wouldn't meet anyone in the kitchen but as she came around the corner, she found Rocco sitting there. The laptop she'd been using on the plane was now sitting on the table before him.

"Morning." He grabbed the insulated coffee pot before him. "Want some coffee?"

"Yes, please." She picked out one of the mugs off the counter and handed it to him. "You're up early."

"I don't sleep much." He poured coffee into her mug before topping off his own. "There's some milk in the fridge and sugar's here, but I'm afraid there's no cream."

"Not to worry; as long as it's hot and strong, I like it black. I've never been much for those girly drinks." She pulled out the chair across from him and sat down.

"That doesn't surprise me one bit." He closed the laptop and pushed it aside. "Has he woken yet?"

"No." She wrapped her hands around the coffee mug, clinging to its warmth. "Doctor Winstead checked in on him before he went to bed and told me that if he needed anything to wake him. Tanner came in too and examined him. What's his role in this? You call him a medic, but what experience and schooling does he have?"

"Tanner's parents are both surgeons and they pushed for him to follow in their footsteps. He attended medical school for two years before his mother was diagnosed with brain cancer. As his mother fought cancer, his father was too busy to be there for her. So Tanner took time off school to be with her and after she passed, he couldn't bring himself to go back. He didn't want to be so busy that he missed his own life."

"So how did he end up working for you?" She took a sip of the coffee.

"I served with his older brother, Travis, and when I attended the funeral, we were introduced. Several months passed before I heard from him again and a couple of days later, he was hired. He's one of my best operatives. I'm hoping that when Travis leaves the service later this year, he'll join Phantom Security, too. I could always use more good men like him on the team."

"Then he knows what he's talking about." Contemplating this, she brought the mug of coffee to her lips and took a sip before sitting it back down. "He told me that the burns are serious but Doctor Winstead's treatment seems to be helping. He didn't find anything alarming about Dad's status and has even convinced Winstead to hold off on the next dose of pain medication so I can speak with him. I know the drugs are keeping him comfortable—but he needs to know I'm here. Maybe it's more that I need the reassurance my father is in there."

"Tanner might not have the title of doctor but he's damn good at what he does. You can trust him. But if you're concerned with Doctor Winstead's ability, I can call Flynn; he'll come and do an exam if that would ease your mind."

"No." She shook her head. "Thank you, I appreciate it, but you've already done so much for me. I guess I worry about Winstead because of the hell his wife put me through. I know he's supposed to be an excellent doctor but suddenly, when it's your family in the bed, supposedly isn't enough."

"I know." He reached across the table and placed his hand over hers. "He's going to be okay and we're going to get through this together. Though if you want me to be honest, I don't think you're worried about his health; I think you want him to wake up because you want his reaction over with."

She stared at him for a moment, doing her best to determine if he meant what she thought he meant or if he was getting at something else. "I…ah…don't know what you mean."

"Flash."

The sound of his name made her glance toward the hallway, as if she could see him still sleeping in the recliner. She'd have given anything to be cuddled in his embrace again, without a care in the world. "Dad's going to flip and while the selfish part of me wants Flash there with me, I know shit's going to hit the fan. I just don't understand why he's against Flash like he is. Dad was irate when he found out we were dating and that was before Flash got into any legal trouble."

"Chief Dalton was protecting you." He pulled his hand away and leaned back.

"From what?"

"He'd seen what our father did to our mother. The abuse she'd suffered through every day until she'd had enough and took her own life. When she did, Dad turned on us. Your dad didn't want that for you and, fearing the worst, he chose to do his best at stopping things between you and Flash before it could happen. Only he didn't know he was too late; you were already in love with Flash."

"He'd never hurt me." She defended him even though she knew she didn't have to. Not with Rocco.

"We know that, but Chief Dalton has seen it too often in his line of work. He did what he thought was right for you." He took a long drink of coffee before returning it to the table and leaning forward. "Flash's past might not be as clean as you might like it to be but the two of you share a love that most people would die for. Don't let it slip away, like I did."

"What happened?" The question slipped out before she could stop it. "Sorry, that's not my business."

The seconds ticked by as silence settled upon them. She sat drinking her coffee, debating how to make things peaceful between them again. Not knowing how, she refilled her coffee cup and rose. "I'll…"

"Unlike with you and Flash, there was no one standing in my way. I had the girl I loved, the one I wanted to marry, and instead of grabbing hold of it with both hands, I let it slip by. I went off to boot camp, like I had always planned. It was my escape from my father. I thought I'd come back and ask her to marry me and we'd move to wherever I was stationed. Only a snowstorm kept me from coming home. She was disappointed, but things were only tense between the two of us until my leave was approved. When my leave got cancelled, that was her breaking point. It didn't matter that I was deploying and had no say in it. She saw it as me disappointing her again and ended things. Now she's married and I'm an old single bachelor."

"You're not old." She sat the mug down and placed her hands on the back of the wooded chair. "I'm sorry that happened, but it was better to know she couldn't live that life before you married her. She wasn't the right woman for you. That lady is still out there, waiting for you to find her. Look at me and Flash. Years later, I was still waiting on him. We found each other just as I know you'll find the woman you're supposed to make Mrs. Rocco Arquette."

He placed his hands in front of him on the table. "I'm not looking for anyone. My life is too busy but hopefully things will calm in the future. Right now, I'd be satisfied with your joining Phantom Security. Unless I'm wrong, you already plan on leaving the FBI, so what do you say?"

"I'd say that your brother is trying to recruit me for his team."

"That little shit!" He dragged his hand through his hair. "All these years you were forbidden and now he swoops in to claim you."

"You did tell me I could hand select anyone I wanted." Flash strolled toward her. "Morning, sweetie, did you get any sleep? Never mind—from the look on your face, I know the answer to that. Go on back; he's starting to wake up."

"Thanks." She arched up onto her toes to kiss him. "You'll come back, won't you?"

"Let me get a cup of coffee and I'll be there." He ran his hand down her back. "Go, sweetie, before I forget where we are and fuck you on this table."

"Fuck, man, you're a pig," Rocco bitched.

"And you're jealous."

"Enough, boys." She reached back to the table to get her coffee. "Rocco, you know I'm an asset to the company no matter whose team I'm working on. Having me work for you is better than me working for the opposition." With that she strolled from the kitchen and headed back to the bedroom to see her father. Their conversation wouldn't be easy, but for once she felt like she was living her life, not just surviving from one day to the next.

Stepping back into the bedroom, she noticed everything appeared the same. The only difference—her father's hand was uncovered. Nearing the bed, she sat her coffee on the bedside table and pulled the chair closer. Preparing herself for the conversation, she took him in. He seemed too pale and the cut above his eye on his forehead seemed too red, as if it should be bleeding. Rationally, she knew it was all an overreaction. She took his hand in hers and his fingers twitched. It could have been a muscle spasm but maybe it was more.

"Dad." His eyes fluttered but didn't open. "Come on, Dad, open your eyes." Moments passed as he tried but the pain medication continued to drag him under. All the hours she sat by his bed waiting for him to wake up were about to pay off. Her stomach churned as she used the time to think about what she'd say to her father. Every possibility she ran through mentally risked invoking more rage from him.

"Eli…se."

"I'm here, Dad." Shaking her thoughts away, she leaned closer to the bed.

"Where have you been?" His voice was clear as though he hadn't still been in a drug induced sleep. "They wouldn't tell me anything. I couldn't get a phone."

"It's okay, Dad. I'm here now." She leaned closer to the bed, doing her best to hide the tears that had fallen. "I'm so glad you're alive…I thought…"

"What?" He took the hand she was holding and brought it to her head, causing her to look up at him. "What happened to you?"

"I'm fine."

"Don't lie to your father." His gaze narrowed on her.

"She was kidnapped and almost killed, but she's safe now." Flash stepped out of the doorway and came to stand next to her.

"What the hell are you doing here, Flash Arquette? I told you to stay away from my daughter."

"Dad, don't. Flash saved my life." She leaned back in the chair and reached up to take Flash's hand. "Shit went to Hell when you were whisked away by the FBI and I received the call you were dead. I left the case I was on in Florida and rushed home. Lewis and Chang arrested Flash on murder charges—your murder."

"He's a likely suspect. If anyone wanted me dead in Pinewood, it would be him."

"Bullshit, Dad." She rose from the chair with such force, it would have knocked over if Flash hadn't been standing there. "He wasn't even in town when your cruiser blew up, but Lewis manufactured the evidence he needed."

"You're going to take his word over that of my department?"

"Yeah, Dad, I am. I've seen the proof. Unlike what you want to believe, I know Flash; he would never have done it. He saved my life from Lewis. That asshole tried to kill you, and he wanted to kill me."

"Come on, sweetie." He placed his hand on the small of her back. "This isn't helping either of you."

"What kind of lies have you been filling her head with?"

"Sir. If I may?" Without waiting for an answer, Rocco strolled into the room. "You might not like us, but we're part of this and like it or not, we're all targets until Chang is arrested."

"It's more than that." She stepped up to the side of the bed and looked down at her father. "Dad, I love you, and when I thought I lost you, something broke within me. Now you're alive but I don't think that part of me is fixable. I lost faith in the system you've stood for your whole life. The people I thought I could trust and depend on betrayed me. First Lewis, when he tried to kill you, then Winstead when she withheld vital information from me and the team. If she'd had it her way, I still wouldn't know you're alive. Finally, one of my own team members, Mick—he had his reasons, but he drugged me and delivered me to Lewis to be killed. I'm done with it. This whole situation cost me too much, but I refuse to lose anything else."

"I don't know what you mean." He reached out to take her hand but she moved away. "Winstead told me you were safe. That's all she would give me but I believed her. We had an agreement. If my cover was blown, you'd be picked up and transported somewhere safe. I knew Lewis would go after you to get to me and I wanted to protect you."

"Assistant Director Winstead failed to keep her end of the bargain," Rocco told him. "She arrived in Pinewood hours after your cruiser was bombed. It wasn't until the following day that her team joined her, after finding out what had happened. On Williams' orders, Jac stood in as Elise's fiancé to act as protection."

"It would seem Assistant Director Winstead failed both of us, but that doesn't matter now. I'm done with the situation, but I'm going to make sure the chain of command knows what happened. But as I started to say, I'm tired of losing. Now I'm going to fight for what I want." She stepped back to stand next to Flash and slid her arm around his waist. "Your actions and hatred cost me Flash once, but I refuse to allow it to happen again. Dad, no matter what you think of him. I love him."

"You can't." Her father's voice rose as he stared at her. "You don't even know who he is."

"You're wrong. I know about his past, everything you wanted to keep hidden. I know his father beat his mother, and that's part of why you tried to keep me away from him." She felt him still under her touch at the mention of his parents. "But there was no reason for that. He would never harm me. He loves me, just as I love him. He was there for me when I needed him, and I know he'll be there in the future. I hope you can accept that but I understand if you can't. Still, it will change nothing."

"You're an FBI agent. You can't date a criminal."

"A lot has changed since you've been away. I'm leaving the FBI and Flash isn't a criminal. His record is clean, something to do with saving the lives of two FBI agents." She leaned into his chest and his arm tightened around her.

"What have you done?"

"Nothing. Flash did all the work, but Dad, even if his record wasn't spotless, I wouldn't let that stand in the way of what we have." She glanced toward Rocco as his earlier words replayed in her thoughts. "This comes around once in a lifetime; well, in our case twice, but you have to grab it with both hands and hold on. Last time I let myself believe what you said and I didn't fight for him. I lost him and now that I have him back, I'm not letting anything stand in our way."

"And your career?" her father pressed. "You're just going to throw it away?"

"No, I'm just allowing it to take me in another direction."

"Elise has accepted a position at Phantom Security." Rocco looked at them before turning back to her father. "You might not believe it, but Flash saved Elise's life and he'll continue to look after her when they're in the field together."

"I think my patient has had enough excitement. It's time for his medication." Doctor Winstead stood in the doorway, clutching a piece of paper in his hand.

"I demand to speak with Assistant Director Winstead." Chief Dalton tipped his head to look at the doctor.

"That would be difficult at the moment." He moved toward the bed and pulled a bottle of pills from his pants. "It seems as though my wife has left."

"She what?" Rocco stepped in the doctor's way. "What do you mean she left? Where did she go?"

"Your guess is as good as mine." He tossed the paper he had been clutching at Rocco. "Seems she received word to report to Director MacArther's office. Rather than face the music, she's running. She left behind her cell phone and when I answered it, I was informed I need to meet with this man now, as well. She's left a mess of trouble behind her and for once, I'm not picking up after her. She can deal with this bullshit herself. However, since I need to go to Washington D.C. now, I'd like to go over instructions with you, Elise. I'd also like to see him transported home to be cared for by his own doctor or at least under another doctor's care before I leave."

Elise wasn't shocked that Assistant Director Winstead had taken the coward's way out and ran but she felt bad for the man who stood before her. He found himself in the middle of the mess she'd created and while his voice was flat as if he didn't care, his eyes told another story. Pain swam in his eyes and his fists were clenched at his side in anger. He had to report to Director

MacArther's office to answer for his wife but he had been told so little before they showed up.

"I'll make arrangements to have him transported. Both Pinewood and New York are out of the question, but I'll see to a safe location where he can heal," Rocco assured Elise before turning back to the doctor. "Doctor Flynn will take over his care. He's worked with me in the past so I don't believe there will be any issues. Also, while you're discussing care instructions with Elise, I'd like to have Tanner sit in. He'll be assisting with Chief Dalton's care until he's back on his feet."

"Very well." He handed the pill bottle to Rocco. "Make sure he takes two of these now. I'll go back and will be in the living room when you're ready." Doctor Winstead left then and Rocco handed her the pills.

"Thanks," she told him as she took the bottle and he went to make the calls.

"When did I become incapable of dealing with things myself?" her father complained.

"Dad, I don't want to fight but right now you need to focus on healing. Rocco's going to make arrangements to have you moved and in a few days, once you're out of the woods, you can go back to Pinewood." She pried open the pill bottle and pulled two out before grabbing the water bottle next to the bed.

"What about you?" He took a sip before holding his hand out for the pills.

"It's likely I'm going to have to make a trip to D.C. as well. I might be done with the FBI but I'm sure they'll have questions for me, and either way I made a promise to Jac that I plan to keep. He's backed me on my quest to find you and I'm going to do my best to make sure he stays out of trouble for it. After that, I'll be in New York."

"Lewis ordered an attack on your house. Bullet holes and a small fire in the living room, so there's damage. Rocco had it secured before we had to get Elise out of town, but no repairs have been made yet." Flash explained. "Craig could oversee things if you'd like for me to have repairs started."

"No," he snapped before popping the pills in his mouth. "Can you give us a minute alone?"

Flash looked at her and she nodded. With a quick kiss to her temple, he walked out of the room, leaving behind an uneasy tension.

"I don't like this, Elise. Not one bit. I taught you better than this."

"You might not be able to see it, but he's a good man." She tried to dispel her father's fear, but nothing seemed to do the trick.

"He's already hit you, hasn't he? I can see the bruises." He eyed the bruise on her face before dropping his gaze to the finger marks on her arm.

"Never. This is from Lewis." She pulled the blanket up around him, tucking him back in. "Please, Dad. I understand this is a shock and you can't accept it right now, but he'd never hurt me. I'm safe with him. He loves me."

"His father claimed to love his wife, but I saw the bruises on her. I picked her limp body up out of the snow after he nearly beat the life out of her. He's violent and it only takes once for his anger to lash out and kill you." He grabbed her hand. "Think, Elise, you know this. You've seen it in your training and in the field. Don't become a statistic."

"I'm not." She pulled her hand away from him. "Now, I've heard enough. Not accepting him is your choice, but I refuse to listen to this. Flash isn't the man his father was, and neither is Rocco...not that you seem to have a problem with him."

"Rocco's proven to me he's different. Every time I have the misfortune to be around Flash, it's in my official capacity."

"Well, Dad, you won't have to worry about that any longer. We can't return to Pinewood, not if we want a fresh start. Everyone there believes Flash is a criminal. Just because he didn't murder you like Lewis tried to convince them, it doesn't mean they'll accept him. His legal issues in the past need to stay there and the problems won't stop if he returns to Pinewood. So you won't have to worry about him being in your town again or any calls concerning him." She stepped away from the bed. "Flash has always been the one topic we disagreed on, but I'm begging you to drop this. I love you but I also love him. Don't make me choose."

She left but instead of going to the living room where everyone waited, she slipped into the bathroom. Her father's words cut through her, leaving her raw, and to pull herself back together, she needed a few minutes alone. The idea that her father hated the man she loved with such passion made her furious. Flash had done nothing to her father to cause such hatred; the actions he was being held responsible for had come from his father. Nothing she said seemed to phase her father. Even knowing that Flash had saved her life wasn't enough. Would he have preferred for Flash to leave her to die? Sitting on the edge of the tub, she leaned forward, burying her face in her hands. Choosing between her father and Flash would cost her almost as much as when she thought he was dead, but she couldn't give Flash up. *Don't I deserve the same chance at happiness as he and mom had?*

Chapter Fourteen

After moving to another house and spending two days in the Poconos, Flash was growing restless. Sitting around waiting for the other shoe to drop wasn't his style and knowing Chang was still on the run made him uneasy. Unless Chang's priorities had changed, he was out there somewhere planning an attack on them in order to eliminate El. Having her in jeopardy made him want to hunt down Chang himself. Maybe going after the bastard would be an excuse to get away from the tension that had engulfed the house.

The uneasiness between El and Chief Dalton was beginning to wear on all of them. Frustrated, El sought comfort in his embrace, making him want to fix things. She was close to her father and this strain between them was killing her. It had gotten to the point where even Tanner and the other two guards that were there with them had picked up the mood and tried to stay out of the way.

Rocco was busy running Phantom Security and had somehow pulled together enough manpower to send a team to back Williams on the search for Chang. It wasn't an official government contract so there would be no payment for their services. He had done it because of El. She might not realize it yet, but she had already become part of the Arquette fucked up family.

Debating his next move, he paced in front of the window. Outside, the world was still. Not a car driving up the road, leaves blowing in the wind, or even an animal scampering off in the distance. He wasn't sure if that was foretelling shit was about to hit the fan or if he was just overthinking things. It made him wonder if they didn't need to leave the area. Moving from the first safe house the Winsteads had to this might not have been enough. He needed to think about keeping El safe, even if it meant taking her away.

"Chief Dalton would like you see you." Tanner dropped down into one of the living room recliners.

"What for?" His question sounded defensive even to his own ears, but Chief Dalton refused to even look at him the few times he had to speak with El.

"He only asked me to fetch you." Tanner rubbed a hand down his face. "That man is becoming unbearable the more we deny his request to return to Pinewood."

"I know, El's been fighting with him about it, but he can't show up in town yet. Williams isn't sure there aren't any others in the police department that are compromised. Chang's the only one left who can answer that and he's in the wind."

"Eventually the risk will have to be taken if he's going to return home." Tanner leaned back in the chair. "It might be better to risk it now than wait."

"You're right." He glanced in Rocco's direction, wanting his input, but his brother was on the phone. "I'll talk to Rocco when he's done with his call and see how he wants to go about this. Dalton is healing and while the burns are still an issue, he's off the pain medication, so he could go home without being under a doctor's care. Craig Freeman might be willing to stay with him and look over him until he's healed."

"If you need me…" Tanner's words died off as if he was asking himself what in the world he was thinking, offering himself up for the job.

"Don't worry, man, you've done enough." With one last glance out the window, he headed to find out what El's father wanted. Whatever the old man had to say, he was sure he wasn't going to like it.

"Good luck," Tanner called.

I'm going to need it. He turned the corner and stepped into the only guest room on the first floor. The room was supposed to be peaceful with its pale blue walls and blue and white decorations scattered around, but the walls seemed to close in on him. He glanced at Chief Dalton, the man who'd played a part in keeping El and him separated. While anger sparked within him, he could also understand where Dalton was coming from. He wanted to protect his daughter, the same way Flash wanted to protect El. They both had her best interest at heart, but she was her own person; she wasn't going to be stifled by either one of them.

"You wanted to see me?" He stayed near the door, partly for a quick exit when the hate started spewing. Staying and dealing with his hatred would only make Flash say or do something that would cause a further rift between El and her father, and that was the last thing he wanted.

"Where's Elise?" Chief Dalton put the book he had been reading aside.

"Resting. It's been a rough week for her and she's exhausted." After finding her in the tub, asleep, he'd forced her to get some sleep. "I'll ask her to stop in when she's awake."

"I could have had Tanner do that. I wanted to see you for other reasons."

Flash waited, hoping he'd continue, but he remained silent. "Are you going to get to the reason? Otherwise, I have things I need to do."

"I want you to stay away from Elise."

"Not going to happen." He crossed his arms over his chest, letting Chief Dalton know the topic was closed. "Anything else?"

"She has a good career and your presence will jeopardize that. If you care about her at all you'd step aside and let her get back to the life she's made. You're no good for her."

"I know she's told you she's leaving the FBI and has accepted a new position with Phantom Security." He swallowed the anger that poured through him and kept his voice level. "You don't have to like the changes she's making both with her job and with me, but I ask that you accept it for her. The tension between you two is stressing her to the max. You're her father and she loves you. When she thought you were dead, she stayed strong because of the insanity surrounding her but her grief was overwhelming. Finding you alive gave her another chance."

"What do you know about it?" Chief Dalton snapped.

"I know that she's always been close with you. When her mother died, that bond became stronger. The day her mother passed she came to me, heartbroken, with tears streaming down her face. I held her while she cried, waiting for her to tell me what had her so upset, and when she could finally speak it came out that she was more worried about you than anything else. Seventeen and about to head off to college, she was terrified she'd lose you, too. The love you and your wife had was strong and with Mrs. Dalton gone, she didn't know what you'd do without her. College was no longer exciting; she wanted to stay home to be with you but you encouraged her to go. Still, she came home every weekend and she kept on doing that to this day."

"What does that have to do with it?"

"That bond is still there. Nothing has changed, at least not for her. Your attitude is ripping her heart out." Flash walked farther into the room, coming to stand near the foot of the bed. "You might not like me and that's fine. You might even believe I'm not good enough for El, which is your right. But what you're doing to her isn't right. I love her and even if you can't see it, I will protect her. Even if that means I have to protect her from you. I walked away from her once because I didn't want to be the divide between the two of you, but the rift is there even if I'm out of the picture."

"You always said you wanted me happy. If you meant it, Dad, you'd accept this because Flash makes me happy." El pulled the cardigan she was wearing tight around her as she stood in the doorway.

"Elise, you don't know what you're asking." Her father shook his head as she strolled toward them.

"I do." She stopped next to Flash and slipped her arm around his waist. "I've spent days trying to convince you to accept this, but I'm done. I can't do it anymore. There's nothing left to say."

"What about your career?"

"I spoke with Williams a few minutes ago. Chang was found dead in his apartment. It's all over. You can go back to Pinewood now. I'll have Rocco make arrangements. During the call, he also informed me that the investigation into my actions and breaking protocol have been dropped. Jac and I are cleared to returned to duty."

Not sure what was coming next, Flash wrapped his arm around her back and let his hand slip underneath the sweater and tank top she wore to rub along her bare skin. She spoke about leaving the FBI, but once the investigation was opened, everything went into standstill mode. Williams had requested that she wait to resign until after she was cleared; otherwise, she'd close off any future possibility of rejoining the bureau and other agents might believe she'd stepped down because she was guilty.

She did violate protocol but she hadn't been the only one. Assistant Director Winstead was in serious trouble but instead of facing it, she was in the wind. It turned out the whole investigation into the prostitution ring and Lewis had occurred off the books. She wanted Lewis for her own reasons. Though, so far, the reasons hadn't been brought to light, at least not to them, and if Williams knew, he wasn't saying.

The silence stretched on until she tipped her head to look at him. As their gazes locked, she smiled, and even though her father was in the room, it was like they were alone. "I've done it. I've put in my resignation, effective immediately."

"You've what?" her father hollered, sitting up straighter in bed. "This is his idea, isn't it?"

"No, Dad." She turned back to look at him. "I started to lose faith in them when they let my team go into a dangerous situation without the necessary information. The connection was severed when they let me believe you were dead. I actually planned your funeral and attended your wake. If I hadn't been kidnapped, I would have buried you. I loved working with the FBI and my colleagues, but my time to leave has come. Two members of my team are dead; it won't be the same. A better and brighter opportunity has presented itself. Working for Phantom Security will still allow me to do everything I love, while not having the doubts about the management. Next time I'm in the field, I'll know I'll have all available information."

"You'll have no power!" He slammed his hand down onto the bed, making the book he had been reading jump. "No doubts about the management? You trust the Arquettes more than the government? This is insane."

"Power was never the reason why I got into law enforcement. I wanted to make the world safer. As for Rocco and Flash, yes, I do. They were there for me when I needed them. I've always trusted Flash and Rocco grew on me. Even if you don't believe it, they're good guys."

"What happens when they send you into a situation that could get you killed? Who's going to be there for you? I trusted Williams and your team to get your ass out alive."

"I shouldn't waste my breath saying this because you won't believe it, but I'll keep her safe. I'd die rather than see her harmed." He pulled her a little tighter to him. "Maybe this will put your mind at ease. Former Special Agent Jac Armiger has accepted a position with Phantom Security as well. He'll be working with El. Jac has protected her in the past and there's no doubt in my mind he'll do it again if he needs to."

"Jac's leaving the FBI?" Her eyes went wide with shock.

"He pulled me aside earlier to see if the job offer was still on the table. I guess what you said hit home." The rest of Jac's life changing decisions needed to come from him, not from Flash, but the changes he was making had been inspired by El's words to him. It made him see that he wasn't living the life he wanted. Hopefully, Phantom Security would give him a better balance.

"Insane!" Dalton took hold of his book but didn't open it yet. "How you can just give up on everything you've worked for is beyond me. My department is in tatters, some of my men were traitors, the whole town thinks I'm dead, but do you see me giving up? No. I'm going to put the pieces together and keep Pinewood safe."

"What about this case you and Lewis were putting together against Flash? Is this something we still need to worry about? Are you going to try to have him arrested on manufactured evidence like Lewis did?" She leaned forward and placed her hand on the bed. "Please don't answer that as the chief of police but as my father."

"If he's arrested, it wouldn't be on manufactured evidence."

"Don't worry, El. There's nothing he can arrest me for." Maybe he was just being hopeful but he had to believe if there had been something in the case they were building against him that he'd still be behind bars.

"You sure about that?" Chief Dalton stared at him, trying his hardest to make Flash second guess what they might have been building, but it wasn't working.

"Yes."

"Dad?" She straightened her back and drove her hand through her hair, all the while shaking her head. "Forget it. I don't know why I expected you to be truthful with me about it. You've never been straightforward with me when it comes to him."

"How do you even know about the case?"

"The day after I received news of your death, I went to your office. I told Lewis I was there to clean it out, but by then I knew things weren't adding up and I wanted to see him. That's when I found this." She pulled a folded piece of paper out of her pocket and went around the side of the bed to hand it to her father.

"What is it?" Flash asked.

"A letter addressed to me, in case something should happen to him. You knew all along that you were in danger but you didn't say anything to me. You let that asshole come to the house each weekend and take part in our family dinner."

"Watch your language, young lady."

"Did you know that asshole was watching me? He has cameras set up all around your house and he looked forward to me coming home each weekend." When he didn't take the letter, she slipped it back into her pocket. "He wanted to fuck me. That's part of the reason he wanted to kill you because he thought I'd seek comfort in his arms. I didn't, because Jac was there pretending to be my fiancé."

"No!" Chief Dalton's voice brimmed with rage as he clenched his fists.

"It's been going on for years. He watched me when I cuddled with Bear on the bed, after he broke his leg." A single tear rolled down her cheek and she dropped into the chair next to the bed. "All that time he watched me, wanting me, but because I dug into your murder, he considered me a liability and was going to kill me."

"Lewis was a lot of things but he thought of you as a daughter," Dalton reasoned.

"That must be why he beat me, slammed me against the wall hard enough that my head bounced off the hard stone, and then he shot me. It was just a grazing wound, but he fucking shot me. Since he couldn't turn me into his wife, he wanted me dead." She shot up from the chair and stepped away. "Defend him if you want but he tried to kill both of us. He's guilty of other deaths, kidnapping, and I could go on—but why, when he's dead? I will say this, one of the last things he said to me before Flash came to my rescue was that you'd rather see me with Arquette than with him. That's why he never made a move before he killed you. So maybe you should be happy that I'm with Flash rather than stuck with someone like that. If it wasn't for Flash, Lewis would have killed me."

She stormed out of the room before Flash could stop her. He paused before following her and looked back at her father. "You might disagree with my actions but killing Lewis was the best I could have done. El is safe and that should be what matters most to you." With that, he turned from Chief Dalton and headed after El. The idea of someone watching her, seeing her naked, and violating her in that way made him livid, but he couldn't let the anger for a dead man overwhelm him, not when she needed him. *I'm coming, El. Nothing like this is ever going to happen again. I'll protect you.*

Chapter Fifteen

The conversation with her father still weighed on Elise's mind hours later, but she refused to go back in there. She couldn't take the tension any longer and while it was only delaying the inevitable, after dinner she cuddled with Flash on the sofa. The guys had some movie in but she wasn't paying enough attention to it to know what it was about.

Rocco seemed to enjoy it while the rest could take it or leave it. In the first twenty minutes of the movie, Tanner was the first casualty, falling asleep. Flash seemed more occupied by her than anything else, making her wish they could slip away upstairs without anyone noticing.

"We can, you know?"

"Huh?" She glanced at Flash.

"Go upstairs." His teeth grazed along her earlobe, making her lean into him. "I saw you glancing in that direction."

"Elise." Her father's voice had her lifting up so she could look over the back of the sofa, only to find him standing in the small entryway that led to the downstairs bathroom and his bedroom. "We need to talk. Bring Flash, too."

She was tempted to say they had nothing to talk about; their differences had been voiced time and time again but he was her father and that alone made her get up. "You don't have to…"

"Not a chance, sweetie." He rose from the sofa and took her hand in his. "We're in this together."

She was grateful to have him by her side, especially since she wasn't sure what this was about. Whatever he intended to say probably wasn't something she wanted to hear, but it was his last chance. In the morning, they'd board a plane to take them back to New York. At the airport, they'd meet with Craig, who was driving up to transport her father back to Pinewood. Since the house Craig had been renting was burned to the ground in retaliation for him going to Elise after Flash was arrested, he would stay with Chief Dalton.

Knowing someone would be with her father eased the guilt of not going home with him. Even if things were different with Flash, she couldn't return home. That house would always serve as a reminder of what Lewis had done. She had no idea where the cameras were but Craig had promised to find them. When he did, she had to know if there were recordings somewhere out there of her. Had anything been found in Lewis's house? Actually, she didn't want to think about that, because it meant someone had watched them to see what they were.

"I was wondering if you'd come."

"No matter our differences, you're my father and I'd come." Shoving her thoughts aside, she looked up to see her father sitting on the edge of the bed. "What's on your mind, Dad?"

"The case." He climbed back onto the bed and pressed his back against the headboard, his gaze on Flash. "You have nothing to worry about. I'll have it destroyed tomorrow."

"Sir?"

"You'd destroy evidence to keep Flash out of jail?" She couldn't believe what she was hearing.

"Manufactured evidence, yes." Dad let out a sigh and shook his head. "Lewis was planning on pinning the missing girls on Flash. Everything in there is stuff he's gathered, but none of it's true. I know because I watched Lewis take the girls in each of the photographs. He knew I was looking into it, so he was covering himself. Flash was an easy target, one he thought I'd be all too happy about pinning them on, especially once two of the girls in the photographs turned up dead."

"Thanks, Dad."

"Don't get me wrong, Elise. I still don't think he's good for you and if there comes a day when he gets locked up, I'll be the first to say I told you so." He looked at each of them before shaking his head. "For your sake, girl, I hope I'm wrong."

"You're wrong about Flash and someday you'll see it." Letting go of Flash's hand, she went to her father. "I know you're not happy with the choices I'm making, but I need a change. I want what you and Mom had. With Flash, I have that."

"I didn't see it, maybe because I didn't want to, but after our earlier discussion I realized that, for you, it's always been him. He looks at you with love and devotion, but all I could see was the way his father looked at his mother. I wanted to protect you; that's all I've ever wanted." He took her hand in his and squeezed it gently. "If you're happy with him, then I'll do my best to accept that. But if I ever find out he's laid a hand on you, I'll kill him."

"I love you, Dad, but you're not a murderer. You'd find a million charges to stick him with, locking him up until he draws his last breath. But killing someone—that's not you." She sank down onto the edge of the bed, next to him.

"You're really going to stay in New York?"

"For now." She blinked away the tears that threatened to fall. "It's not that far. You can see me anytime you'd like."

"But you won't be coming home." The sadness in his voice sliced at her heart.

"Not until you make sure your department is clean and she's in no danger. Craig's going to search every square inch of your house to make sure he's got the cameras Lewis placed there. After that, we can discuss it." Flash came up behind her and placed his hand on her shoulder. "But after everything that's happened, she won't be coming alone. Tanner or Jac can accompany her. It's not that you can't keep her safe, but you can't be with her every minute. As the chief of police, you can be called out at any time."

"I can protect myself." She started to turn enough to take Flash in, but her father spoke, stopping her.

"He's right."

"Alpha men are going to be the death of me. Did you both forget that I'm...was...a trained FBI agent. I can handle myself." With a cocky grin, she met her father's gaze. "I bet I can out shoot both of you."

"No way. I'm ashamed to admit it, but it was too close last time. I'm not taking that chance again." Dad shook his head as a smile spread over his face. "Seriously, Elise, I agree with Flash on this. I knew Lewis was dirty, which is why, when Winstead approached me about working with her, I agreed. I wanted to take him down and that was the easiest way. But Officer Chang, I never suspected him."

"Don't blame yourself. They had me fooled, too." Even now, when she looked back at it, she didn't see anything abnormal; nothing hinted at the other life Lewis lived, or even at his attraction to her.

"Give me time, Flash, and you'll be able to come with her if you want." Dad stifled a yawn and she realized the dark circles under his eyes were getting darker. He needed sleep. "I'm going to make sure everyone knows what you did and how you saved Elise's life. I'm going to clear your name, allowing you to have the start you should have had. No one, myself included, should have held what happened between your parents against you. Then you can come home with her."

"I appreciate that, sir, but I don't think even you have enough power to convince the residents of Pinewood I'm not everything they think I am." His hand still resting on her shoulder, he reached up and brushed his thumb along her cheekbone. "I won't hold El back from coming to see you. I don't want to stand between you two."

"I appreciate that, because she's all I have left. Do you still have that letter?" When she nodded, he continued, "Everything in it is true. Mom and I tried so hard to have a child and when you finally came along, we became a complete family. You were the bright spot in our lives. My little girl, my gun toting, bad-guy-catching princess. Even as a little girl, you knew what you wanted to do and you did it. Even if I chuckled at you catching your imaginary bad guys while dressed in your princess dress and those blue sparkly shoes."

"Now I've traded in my dress and sparkly shoes for a real gun and good boots."

"Don't forget a good computer," Dad teased. "You were always able to find everything there was on a person with just a few clicks. I don't like that you broke procedure, but I knew something was off when Winstead wouldn't tell me anything. She said you were safe, but wouldn't allow me to call you."

"That's why they were keeping you on the pain medication. I know you were in pain so Doctor Winstead had to give you something, but she talked him into keeping you sedated so you wouldn't cause a fuss."

"What I don't understand is: if they told you I was dead, why were you looking for me?"

"Because El here isn't a believer until she sees it with her own eyes." Flash squeezed her shoulder.

"Little things started to add up that didn't seem right, making me question your death. Then, at the funeral home, against everyone's wishes, I had to open the coffin. I had to see. In my mind, I'd know if it was you but in reality, if it was, I wouldn't have known. Agent Bryne's body was extremely burned; even if I had known him I wouldn't have recognized him. Jac caught the height difference. It stood out to him because you're taller than him and he's six one, yet the autopsy said five foot eleven."

"It could have been a misprint," Dad reasoned.

"It wasn't. You were alive. If it makes you feel better, I wasn't completely convinced because of that. I still needed actual proof."

"That's when Rocco produced an image from Doctor Flynn's security system as they were rolling you in," Flash explained. "Thirty minutes later, we were boarding a plane to the Poconos."

"All your life you've questioned everything. No matter how small the detail is, you don't miss it. If it isn't as you expected, you sink your claws into it." Grinning, Dad shook his head. "There were times when that quality could be annoying. Like when you were five and started to question Santa Claus making it to every house all around the world in one night. No matter what explanation I gave you, it didn't work. To your mom, that was the start of you losing your innocence."

"That explains why I saw her crying." In her mind, she could see her mother tucking her into bed that night and as she turned away, the adorable crown nightlight Dad had bought her was just enough light to see her mother's face. There, in the dim light, tears streaked down her mom's cheeks. "I miss her so much."

"Me, too." With his hand in hers, he pulled her toward him so he could wrap his arms around her. "When we married at eighteen, I thought I'd spend the rest of my life with her. I never thought she'd die and leave me alone to raise you. She'd be proud of the woman you are. Your strong, take no shit attitude comes from her. Did you know that her father didn't approve of me either?"

"Granddad—really? I remember you two sitting on the porch drinking a beer and talking about things you wouldn't allow me to hear. You always sent me back in the house." She leaned out of the hug and as she settled back into the chair, Flash's hand returned.

"It took time, but when you came along, that's when things got better between us. After we were married, your grandmother helped to keep him from bitching." He looked at Flash. "I don't know if we'll ever get there, but I'll try as long as you treat my little girl right. She might be all grown up now, but she's my little princess. If you lay a hand on her in anger, there will be hell to pay."

"You don't have to worry about that, sir. She's everything to me." Flash teased his arm down her shoulder.

"Still trying to go all papa bear protective."

"Every day until I'm put in the ground." He tipped his head toward the door. "Now go on. We've got an early morning tomorrow and I need my sleep. There's a lot to do in Pinewood and my police department needs to be whipped back into shape."

Leaving his bedroom, she headed toward the kitchen for a drink. The thought there'd be a funeral for her father one day weighed on her mind. Losing him once was enough to make her cherish their time together and the memories they'd made. Death was a part of life but the day he died, she'd be alone. With both her parents gone and her being the only child, there'd be nobody left as there were no aunts or uncles. She had no siblings. In the end, it would just be her.

"I want you naked and screaming my name." Flash wrapped his arms around her and nuzzled her neck, teasing light kisses as he did. "Let's go upstairs."

"You think I'm just going to drop everything to give you a quick fuck." She kept her hands on the cool granite counter top, denying herself the opportunity to reach between them and cup his hardened cock pressed against her lower back.

"Who said anything about quick?" he grazed his teeth over her earlobe. "Maybe I'll have you moaning all night long, keeping everyone up."

"Promises, promises," she teased.

"You won't be saying that in the morning." He slid his hand up her thigh before lifting the material of her dress and sliding it up further. "No panties. Fuck, El, that's so damn sexy. I could just lift your dress up and shove my dick into your wet pussy."

"Everyone's right in the next room." She kept her voice low as his fingers slipped between her folds and brushed along her clit. "Flash…"

"Yes, sweetie?" His voice sounded innocent but his fingers sped, nearly buckling her knees.

"I'm torn between wanting to you continue and wanting you to stop." She pressed her hand to her mouth, fighting back a moan. "Can't…not…here…upstairs."

"A few sweet strokes and you're mine." He kissed her neck one final time before sliding his hand away.

It took her a moment to speak, her body still on edge from being denied what she so badly needed. "I've always been yours."

"And you always will be." Scooping her into his arms, he headed for the stairs. "We belong together."

"Like a two-piece puzzle." Tenderly, she brushed her fingertips along the curve of his neck then along the edges of his hair. "Together at last."

Rocco insisted they take the master bedroom, giving them a little privacy, but she couldn't wait until they were back in New York. They might have to find a hotel for a few days while they looked for something, but at least they wouldn't have to worry about anyone overhearing. In the master bedroom, he went straight for the bed where he laid her down and stepped back.

"Where are you going?"

"Should I be jealous that you were wearing a dress without any panties? Anyone could have seen your sweet pussy."

"It's not like I'm two again, lifting my dress so everyone can see. I outgrew that, baby. No one gets to see what's underneath but you." She held her hand out to him. "The easy access was for you and if you remember I was cuddled under a blanket downstairs."

"Shit, El, if I'd have known you were naked under that dress I'd have made you climax right there and you'd have had to be quiet unless you wanted everyone to know what was going on."

"You've got a naughty side but you know I can't be quiet."

"And I love that." He pulled his shirt over his head and tossed it to the end of the bed. "On second thought, I think I like the idea of you naked under your dress. You'll have to wear them more often."

"Doubtful. Dresses aren't designed for carrying guns and I feel naked when I'm unarmed. I only left my weapon up here because you're here with me and we're surrounded by Rocco's guys. If one of you can't take down whatever threat is against us, you'll at least buy me enough time to get my gun." She grabbed the bottom of the dress and pulled it up and over her head in one quick move. "Now, once we find a place of our own, I might be persuaded to wear a dress for you. I can see me bent over the counter with you fucking me. Oh damn, Flash."

"Does that turn you on baby?" Stripping off the last of his clothes, he came toward her.

"With you, yes." She sucked her bottom lip between her teeth and as she let it go, she let out a deep hiss. "You've got more weight with Rocco. Once we find a place, can you convince him to give us a couple of days off? I think we need to move into our place the right way."

"What's the right way?"

"Sex in every room and on every surface, of course." She wiggled her eyebrows at him. "Come on, you can't tell me you don't want it as much as I do. To have me bent over the counter or in the shower. None of that turns you on?"

"You know it does, El. I want you everywhere I can get you." He climbed onto the bed next to her. "Let's start tomorrow."

"Huh?"

"The floor below Rocco's penthouse is his, too. It's two condos which he uses for his employees when needed or visitors. He gave me the keys for one today. If you want to find somewhere else, we can but it will be convenient for our offices at Phantom Security. All we'll have to do is take an elevator ride down—which leaves us more time for other activities in the morning. After all you know what they say about morning nooky."

"Nooky? Who even says that anymore?"

"Me," he growled, pushing her back on the bed as he slid on top of her. She spread her legs, welcoming him, before running her foot along the back of his calves. His lips claimed hers and in a frenzy of passion and need, his tongue slid between her lips.

Wrapping her fingers around his shaft, she broke the kiss but didn't move away from him. "So hard and ready. I want this…I want you inside of me."

"So demanding." He kissed her softly before drawing her bottom lip between his teeth and nipping lightly before letting go again. "It's a good thing I love you or your demanding attitude might get you in trouble."

"Really now? I laugh at trouble." She gave him her best impression of a deep, evil laugh.

He dipped his head and his lips wrapped around her nipple but as she felt his teeth graze across the sensitive bud, her body stilled. Biting down with just enough pressure to have her arching into him, he chuckled. "I thought you laughed at danger."

His chuckle made his cock brush along her pussy, making her quiver. Since he came back into her life it was like her body was trying to make up for all the time they had been apart. She was constantly on edge, needing the intimacy with him. The teasing touch of his cock was enough to break her. She couldn't wait any longer; she needed him. "Flash, please…"

"Don't worry, sweetie, I'm going to take care of you." He trailed his hand down her body and between her thighs. The caresses of his fingers had her spreading her legs, and her breath caught in her chest. He explored up her inner thigh, ever so slowly, until he could slip his finger between her folds, quickly finding her center and working deep within her. She moaned as he worked a second finger into her. In and out, quicker with every pump. He thrust into her with his fingers as his thumb teased over her clit, wringing pleasure from her. As her climax approached, he slowed, until he stopped altogether.

"I can't. Please Flash, I want you. Don't make me wait anymore," she murmured holding onto him as wild delight eddied through her.

Even as she wiggled against him, wanting more, he took his time. Easing his way back up the length of her body, he blazed a trail of kisses across her stomach, stroking his fingertips along the curves of her sides. With every touch, she arched her hips into him, demanding more. Yearning coursed through her; she could wait no longer for him to claim her. Her mind lingered in a sexual haze, needing him now.

"Tonight, I want you to ride me. I want to see your tits bouncing as you ride my cock for all it's worth." With his hands on her hips, he rolled off her and onto his back all the while taking her with him.

"I don't think you've ever given me control." Not wanting to miss the opportunity she slid down further, forcing him to open his legs and allow her between them. Her hand slid along the length of his cock, up and down.

"El?" He tried to pull her back up to him.

"I want to taste you." She leaned forward, kissing the tip of him before letting him slip between her lips. Slowly, she started to work her way down his length, taking more and more of him in her mouth. She wasn't sure how much she could take before her gag reflex kicked in. Her hand worked at the base, and he tangled his hand in the strands of her hair. He wasn't pressing her down onto his cock yet, just holding her close. Her mouth worked up and down the length of him, milking the life out of him.

As her pace increased, he moaned and his fingers tangled in her hair. "Fuck, El." She eased up for a moment, slowly coming off him so she could circle her tongue about the tip of him before working back down his length again. Pressing her head down he urged her to take more of him before letting out a deep moan. "That feels so fucking good. But tonight, I want to be in your wet pussy."

She let him slip from her mouth and he pulled her up, so she was once again straddling him. But he didn't stop there; he kept his hand on her back, pressing down on her and encouraging her to lean down to him. When she did, he kissed her neck, nibbling down her jawline to her shoulder. She let him have a few more minutes of exploration, since he'd finally made it to her breasts. He wrapped his mouth around her nipple, flicking his tongue over the bud, drawing it to full hardness. Then, he teased over the other one, tweaking it until it stood at attention. Her nipples had always been extra sensitive, the slightest touch bringing her pleasure. She moaned in ecstasy when his tongue flicked over one hardened tip.

"Now, El." He ordered but did nothing to urge her to move faster.

Desperate, she shifted her position, forcing him to let go of her breast. Angling the head of his cock just below her opening, she sank down onto it, slowly allowing his hardness to fill her inch by inch, until his low moan echoed hers. Obviously not done with her nipples, he reached out and pinched the bud, the pain mingling with pleasure. She rocked upward and then down again, finding her rhythm. Impatience coiled through her as she tried to find the right motion. As if realizing her frustration, he grasped her hips, increasing his pace and driving into her with force.

With every thrust, he sped his pace, hands on her hips, pulling her down onto him harder and faster. Stroke after stroke, the tempo between them intensified until his hips where slamming off hers. The thrusts became deeper, more urgent, falling into a perfect rhythm. Their bodies rocked back and forth and her back arched, pushing her breasts out toward him as her orgasm neared.

The tension strained through her muscles, tightening around his cock.

"Fuck, El." He dug his fingers into her hips. "Tighten around my cock."

As she pushed down onto him, he arched up to meet her. Ever faster and deeper, they met each other's thrusts. They climbed the mountain, both seeking the apex. Her hand landed on his chest, near the puzzle piece tattoo, as her world shattered.

"Flash!" Screaming his name, she slammed down onto his body as her orgasm found her. She dragged her nails along his chest, leaving angry red scratches.

His grasp on her hips tightened, keeping his cock buried deep within her when his own orgasm hit him. "Fuck, baby."

She collapsed on top of him, her hands on either side of him, holding him tight to her. All those years she thought she'd never see him again, let alone actually have him in bed again, and now, she had him.

"Damn, sweetie, I might have to let you ride me more. The gentle bounce as I've got my hands full of your breasts and the tightness of your pussy wrapped around my dick is out of this world." He brushed her hair away from her face.

Her nipples still tingled at the memory of him biting them. The pain brought pleasure mixing to send her over the edge. He had a way of giving her everything she didn't know she needed and craved. His cock twitched inside her, sending a jolt of desire rushing back through her, forcing her inner core muscles to tighten around him again. Damn if she didn't want him again.

"I love it when you do that."

She slipped off him to cuddle beside him, her fingers teasing along his chest. "I might be able to get used to this."

"Good because we've got a lot of time to make up for." He slid his arm under her head and pressed his hand along her back, snuggling her closer to him. "You always believed I was better than the road I took and my actions. Now I'll have the rest of my life to prove it to you. I love you, El."

"You have nothing to prove. Not to me. I love you." She caressed the side of his face, the stubble from days without shaving gone, giving him a smooth finish. It would take a bit of getting used to because she was partial to his slightly rugged appearance. Clean shaved made her want to see him in a suit. *Fucking me on his desk, with the landscape of New York City right outside the window.*

Epilogue

Life had spun on its axis, giving Flash a complete turnaround. Even in his wildest dreams, he'd never expected to be where he was. With no criminal record, he was able to take a position full time with Phantom Security. While his new career beat the hell out of his former criminal lifestyle, it wasn't the reason for his happiness. That was all El. She made him feel like a new man.

When they'd first moved into the condo, he waited for her to wake up one morning and decide it was all a big mistake. He waited for the regret to hit her, over their reconciled relationship, moving in together, and leaving the FBI. Yet it hadn't happened. Two months wasn't a lot of time in the scheme of things, but they were closer now than they had ever been and she seemed to love her work. Even as he waited for the regret to present itself, he hoped it wouldn't. He wasn't sure he could lose her again without losing his mind. To him, they belonged together and the years they were apart, he hadn't been living. He didn't want to go back to that existence.

Standing by the floor to ceiling windows in the bedroom, he stared out at the lights of New York. Eleven o'clock at night but the city was alive. Unlike in Pinewood, where everything was quiet at that time of night, New York was bustling. The city that never sleeps. Living there was like a whole new world. One they had explored a little, but most of their downtime had been enjoyed together in their condo instead. Just as El wanted, they had made love on every surface and in every room. It didn't matter how many times they had sex, it was always new and exciting. The love they shared was unlike anything he'd ever experienced before.

Heels clicked against the hardwood floor as El made her way toward the master bedroom. "Flash?"

"In here." He turned away from the window, grabbed one of the glasses of champagne from the dresser, and went to her.

"What's this all about?" Eyeing him suspiciously, she took the glass from him.

"Celebration of our successful first mission as a team." At least, that had been his reason when he planned this. Now he was thinking it was more than that. "Jac, Tanner, and Burkhart work well together."

"You've picked a good team."

"We," he corrected. "Who'd have thought Jac would request to work under my lead? I know you two are close, but I thought he'd have wanted a different leader."

"I know you two have become good buddies so don't give me any of that bullshit about him not wanting you to lead because of your past. Remember we decided to leave it where it's meant to be, in the past. We're starting our lives fresh and no one needs to know what happened before."

"It's part of me, it's made me into who I am." He stared down at her for a moment, taking her in. "Are you embarrassed by it? Is that why you don't want anyone to know I'm a criminal?"

"You're not a criminal, not anymore. Your record is clean. You made some choices that sent you to prison and I'm very much aware it changed you into who you are now and I'm not embarrassed by it. Not at all. I only meant you have a chance some would give their life for, a clean slate—don't waste it." She took a sip of the champagne and took a step closer to him. "If I was ashamed of it I wouldn't have been planning to be with you even if that meant I had to leave the FBI. Flash, I never stopped loving you and I didn't want to lose you again."

"Oh, El." He slipped his arm around her waist and pulled her against his body. "You're never going to lose me."

"I still remember seeing you shackled and in that horrible orange jumpsuit. I knew you were innocent, but standing there I never felt so helpless in all my life. Jac had to drive me home because I was in a daze—terrified that I'd fail to prove what I already knew was the truth and you'd spend your life behind bars or worse…"

"Shhh sweetie, it's okay." He took her glass and sat it back on the dresser. "It's all over now. You have me now and forever."

"Forever." The word came out on a whisper as she leaned against him, clinging to him.

"Marry me, El." The words were out before he could stop himself.

"What?" She pulled her head away from his chest to look up at him.

"I've been planning this for weeks and I fuck it up."

"No." As she spoke, he started to pull further away, crushed that she said no, but she grabbed the top of his dress slacks, keeping him close. "Don't pull away from me."

"Don't make this worse." Instead of being happy with what they had, he wanted more. He wanted her as Mrs. Flash Arquette. *If I kept my mouth shut, I wouldn't be about to lose her.*

"I didn't say no to your question; I meant no you weren't fucking it up." She let go of his waistband and took his tie into her fists, pulling him down until his face hovered next to hers. "I wasn't sure I heard you right before…say it again."

Looking into her eyes, he tried to figure out what her answer would be. All he could see was how the green sparkled every time she looked at him. It made him think of when they made love, the dreaminess that had her staring into his eyes.

"Say it again." She repeated her words with a little more emphasis.

"Elise Marie Dalton, will you marry me?" His heart pounded against his chest as the seconds ticked by like minutes.

"Yes." Wrapping her arms around his neck, she pressed her lips to his—a simple kiss before she pulled back to look at him again. "You're all I've ever wanted and since you've come back into my life, I've never been happier. I would be honored to be your wife, but you get to tell my father."

"Don't worry, sweetie, that's already taken care of."

"What do you mean, 'taken care of'?"

"When Craig and Chief Dalton visited before we left for the mission, I spoke to him about my intentions. Considering how bumpy things have been, I didn't expect to get his blessing but he surprised me. He sees how happy you are and he wants the best for you." He slipped the ring box from his pocket, opened it, and pulled out the princess cut diamond ring.

"How long have you been carrying that around?"

"Off and on for the last couple weeks, waiting for the perfect moment." He held the ring out, waiting for her finger. "While Rocco had you meeting who knows who, I snuck up here to get things ready. I hadn't wanted to go to the party—too many big names and government officials—but tonight with you was amazing. You worked the room like you owned the place. Rocco needs someone like that as a business partner, not me. I'm not good at that side of things."

"Because every time you look at someone in law enforcement you're reminded of the corruption that goes on. You think they look at you like you're a suspect, sizing you up, but they're not." He slid the ring onto her finger and she took hold of his hand. "It will get easier. Rocco doesn't have any problem with that. He's a social butterfly and a damn good schmoozer. You have other benefits."

"Really, sweetie, maybe I should show you what those are."

"I didn't mean those benefits, though I think celebration sex is in order. I meant you're a great leader; your drive keeps you focused on the mission at hand. Your problem-solving abilities are out of this world. You think of things that would take others longer to get to. I watched you lead the team on this mission and you came out of it alive. You encourage the others to think outside of the box and not to discount anything until it's completely ruled out. More than that, Rocco trusts you to lead the team through shit and bring everyone home safely."

"When you put it that way, maybe he did make a good choice." He reached around her, quickly finding the zipper at the back of her dress. "Now how about that celebration sex." He eased the thin straps down her shoulders.

"I think that can be arranged. After all, that's been my plan all night." She let the dress drop to the floor to reveal she was naked underneath the blue silky material.

"Just like our last night in the Poconos, you're not wearing any panties." He lifted her into his arms and she wrapped her legs around his waist as he pressed her back against the wall. "Never knowing what to expect from you keeps me on my toes, so I know the rest of our lives are going to be anything but boring. You're all I need in my life."

"You wouldn't want to live a boring, normal life, so I'm not worried. Plus, you love me just as I love you—that's what matters," she whispered before pressing her lips to his.

In that moment, everything came together. His life had been full of shadows and for a while, that had cost him the very person that was most important to him. Now that she was back in his life, he vowed to cast out the shadows and live every day proving he could be the man she needed. He'd screwed up before and almost lost his life for a crime he didn't commit, but as she was constantly reminding him, it was the past. They were about to start their life as a married couple and he would put the past behind him once and for all.

"Here's to tomorrow and every day that you're by my side. I love you, El."

Marissa Dobson

Born and raised in the Pittsburgh, Pennsylvania area, Marissa Dobson now resides about an hour from Washington, D.C. She's a lady who likes to keep busy, and is always busy doing something. With two different college degrees, she believes you are never done learning.

Being the first daughter to an avid reader, this gave her the advantage of learning to read at a young age. Since learning to read she has always had her nose in a book. It wasn't until she was a teenager that she started writing down the stories she came up with.

Marissa is blessed with a wonderful supportive husband, Thomas. He's her other half and allows her to stay home and pursue her writing. He puts up with all her quirks and listens to her brainstorm in the middle of the night.

Her writing buddy Pup Cameron, a cocker spaniel, is always around to listen to her bounce ideas off him. He might not be able to answer, but he's helpful in his own way.

She loves to hear from readers so send her an email at marissa@marissadobson.com or visit her online at http://www.marissadobson.com.

Also by Marissa Dobson

Alaskan Tigers:

Tiger Time

The Tiger's Heart

Tigress for Two

Night with a Tiger

Trusting a Tiger

Alaskan Tigers Box Set Vol. 1

Jinx's Mate

Two for Protection

Bearing Secrets

Tiger Tracks

Healing the Clan

Alaskan Tigers Box Set Vol. 2

Her Black Tiger

Tiger Trouble

Forever Creek Shifters:

Forever Fight

Protecting Forever

Crimson Hollow:

Romancing the Fox

Loving the Bears

A Lion's Chance

Swift Move

Purrable Lion

Bearly Alive

Saved by a Lion

Furever Mated Box Set

Stormkin:

Storm Queen

Reaper:

A Touch of Death

SEALed for You:

Ace in the Hole

Explosive Passion

Operation Family